Mississippi Justice: Guilty Until Proven Innocent!

Joe Ruff's Exceptional Life, Volume 2

P.T. "Doc" Carney

Published by P.T. "Doc" Carney & Eva Carney, 2018.

Mississippi Justice: Guilty Until Proven Innocent

First edition. June 2018

Copyright © 2018 P.T. "Doc" Carney.

ISBN: 978-1732208445

Written by P.T. "Doc" Carney.

Cover Design by Tiffany Fox

Editing by Eva Carney

.

CONTENTS

PROLOGUE

The State of Mississippi took two months to review all Dr. Ruff's charts dating back to when he first started his psychiatric practice. In all that time they found a total of 30 instances where there was a charge made but no progress note was written in the patient's chart. And of course everyone knows that any doctor can forget to write a note on occasion. Not to mention that this Attorney General plays to the bible thumping base; who are honest people, good people; but people who don't understand the situation or the law and are being taken advantage of by an Attorney General who is totally without morals or scruples.

Now what was the doctor charged with? He was charged with **30 FELONY** counts for billing a patient without having seen them; **felony meaning, you can go to prison for this**. Now how did this all come about?

Chapter 1
Joe returns to Tucson and Lisa

BY AGE 26, YOUNG JOE Ruff had lived a life of surprise and some-times regret at every turn. At this point he had attended college, gone into the USAF as a jet pilot, fought in the Bay of Pigs invasion and had married and divorced from a horrible marriage. In the meantime though he met his lifelong, longed for partner for life from Great Falls, Montana.

Joe finally deciphered from all this that though he seemed to be a slow learner about some things, especially those about the nature of humans, that once he learned a lesson, he didn't forget and he used it for gain in future encounters. It seemed to him that maybe it wasn't so much the kind or number of mistakes that one makes in life as it was what he had learned from them.

Now he had called Lisa back after 2 1/2 years and it seemed that she had the same resolve because when she answered she said, **"I've been waiting for your call."** She continued, "That is to say, we have both learned from the past what not to do so let's see now if we can get it right." He hoped he was packing and loading his things for the trip to Montana for the last time. When he had spoken to Lisa on the phone last night, she didn't ask any details of why he hadn't called her for 2 1/2 years. She just said that she was happy he had called. She was obvious-ly the kind of woman who knew what she wanted and was willing to wait for it; and he hoped she was committed.

Joe closed out all his remaining business in Tucson and had re-signed at Hughes Aircraft as their Project Engineer. Joe had sold all his motorcycles except for one, his Triumph TR6, and would just pull it on its trailer behind the Chevy convertible. Everything was paid for and he had a few dollars in his pocket. He had not told Lisa about the Amanda Locus marriage. He thought that better done in person and if there was an insurmountable problem about it, he would just get back in the car and keep driving until the urge to stop overcame the urge to keep dri-ving. He knew he had made a serious life blunder but there was nothing for him to do now but keep moving on until he found stability in his life. If he knew Lisa though, she would hear him out and hopefully the two of them could move on TOGETHER.

Certainly his wounds were not yet healed from the plane crash, but he hoped with continued exercise therapy they would heal. How-ever, the CIA had been really good about helping with the bills. He still had bad dreams about the Cuban fiasco and how he and his friends had been abandoned by President John Kennedy in the middle of the Cuban Invasion and how many of the lives of his friends could have been saved if Kennedy had kept his word and supported them with the jet fighter support from the two carriers sitting 2 miles off the coast of Cuba. Your word is your bond had always been his watchword. Joe and the group of eight B26s had lost 4 of 8 aircraft and crews on the first two passes at the beach before the attack was called off. It seems the on-ly lives politicians cherish are their own.

It was a beautiful June day and not hot for a change, so Joe chose to leave the old Pueblo, (Tucson), with the top down. He drove all day and when he approached the Cottonwood, Arizona exit he couldn't help but flash back to the terrible auto accident he had seen and helped with on his last trip to Montana. He wondered about the wife of the man who had been killed in the accident and how she was doing. He was in no great hurry, so he just had it on slow cruise. He followed the same route north that he had taken before, up through Phoenix,

Flagstaff, to Salt Lake City, Butte, MT and on into Great Falls. It would be two long days or three short ones. He was on no particular schedule. Joe was a serious thinker and he kept doing inventories of his life so far and the mistakes he had made and how they had affected his life to this point. But what he really wanted most was to learn from life and then move on forward.

On the third day Joe called Lisa and told her that he was about an hour out of Great Falls. He would get there about noon. She said "Wonderful, come to Dad's office and we will go to lunch at a place where it is quiet and they have booths for more privacy so we can talk." Joe said, "Great." And an hour later he was at her Dad's office and after the kisses and hugs they headed to the Blue Canoe for lunch. They sat down, both on the same side of the booth, and after they ordered he told her the whole Amanda Locos story and all the details, no holds barred, as truthfully as he knew how. Then she smiled and said, "I still love you completely, spots and all. We all make mistakes and that's what life is about. You make mistakes and then you hopefully learn from them. We are all human and as long as that is the case we are going to make mistakes. Joe the biggest thing we have going for us is our honesty with each other and the ability to forgive and move on. Sure the Amanda affair was a mistake for you, but you see that now and you are wiser for it. As for myself, I told you about the mistake I made of marrying my high school sweetheart and what a disaster it was. But our life together begins here and now." Joe was looking her straight in the eyes and kissed her just as the waiter cleared his throat.

They enjoyed a wonderful lunch and later they arrived at Lisa's home. Joe and Lisa unloaded all his belongings and then they unloaded the bike and parked it in the garage. Shortly thereafter they drove to her Dad's home where they waited for him to get home from the office. He arrived promptly at 5:30, as he usually did. Joe and Lisa sat down in the parlor with him and a little small talk was followed by Joe asking him for his permission to marry his daughter. Her Dad seem both surprised and elated. He then asked when this proud event should occur and looked at the two of them.

Lisa said, "It will probably take a couple of months to get all the things done, invitations etc. We must decide where to hold the wedding. There are lots of things to think about. I'll make a list and work on all the details." After that her Dad offered his congratulations and they had dinner. Then Lisa and Joe headed back to her place. Since they had to go through town anyway they stopped by the piano bar, had a few drinks, a couple of dances, and then headed home to Lisa's.

On the way home, Lisa said, "There is so much to do, where to have it and how many invitations. I plan to do this only once so I want it with all the pomp and circumstance it deserves." Joe said, "Right on." Lisa would have a maid of honor and 4 bridesmaids and Joe would have a best man and four groomsmen. There would be a ring bearer, the preacher and her Dad. "That about covers the participants," Lisa said, "Then there is where to have it. I will send out about 300 invitations, including Dad's law partners so where will we have it? That will take up a lot of room. Maybe one of the downtown hotels, we shall see." Lisa then asked, "Who will you want for your best man and groomsman?" Joe said, "Well, Bern my old motorcycle buddy and 3 of the guys that flew in the Cuban invasion with me who didn't get shot down, in fact the only three. Oh yes, and my brother, who is ten years my younger, if he can be here."

As soon as they were home Lisa started making a list for invitations and bridesmaids and began looking at possible places to have the wedding. Then she said, "Oh yes, and then there is the matter of where we will honeymoon, but that can wait. No pressing decision on that yet. Macau, which is China's version of Las Vegas, Singapore, Bali or Hong Kong come to mind. What do you think Joe?" Joe said, "I think we still have time on that one but those are good ideas."

It was July 15th now and the wedding was planned for September 15th. Lisa was contacting bridesmaids who were mostly friends from college and Joe contacted Bern, his old friend from the motorcycle group, to be his best man and he contacted his younger brother, Jack, and the 3 pilots from the Bay of Pigs invasion to be groomsmen. This was a whole new experience for Joe since his only experience had been the shotgun wedding of sorts to Amanda. Lisa looked at all the hotels in the local area and decided on the Hilton Gardens in Great Falls. Also invited were Joe's parents and Joe was anxious for them to meet Lisa, especially his mother.

Joe and Lisa talked at length about their plans after the wedding and the honeymoon and decided to wait until after the wedding to decide on long range plans, but she was aware and approving of his thoughts of going into medicine and the fact that Montana did not have a medical school but the University of Mississippi did. So they continued to make their plans and slowly but surely things were beginning to come together.

Joe's best man, Bern Scales, had been his pit crewman during the years that he raced motorcycles. Bern was just a good old boy who had a 6th grade education and was a painter by trade; but he was an expert at motorcycle stuff. He was really Joe's best friend over the years and there wasn't anything Bern wouldn't do for Joe, so they were thick as hair on a dog's back. He had agreed to be Joe's the best man. Also the groomsmen were going to be Joe's kid brother, who was now only about 16, and he and Joe had always adored each other, and the three surviving pilots of the Cuban Bay of Pigs invasion, Cody Redwine, who was from Great Falls, Montana, Larry Smert of Charleston S C., and John Demond from New Orleans, LA. There is nothing quite like military combat to bring a group of guys close together. It hurt Joe every time he thought about only 4 of the original 8 B26 pilots surviving the invasion attempt.

When President John Kennedy reneged on his support for air cover with 150 A4 fighter jets he had sitting 2 miles off the Cuban coast, that spelled sudden death for the B26 pilots who were heavily armed but had little defense against Castro's ground forces, which became solely concentrated on them. With no cover from the A4s, the B26s were left as sitting ducks. If the carrier jets had done their part in flying cover for the B26s then there would have been a totally different outcome. As it was, the B26 mission was called off after the 2nd pass during which Joe was shot down. They lost 4 B26s in two passes on the target area. Anyway, Joe wanted those other three B26 pilots to be his groomsmen and they had gladly accepted the invitation. In fact, since Cody Redwine was from Great Falls, he and Joe had plenty of social contact over the two months leading up to the wedding.

In the meantime, Lisa had sent out 315 invitations and Phyllis, one of her closest college friends, also from Great falls, would be her maid of honor. She had 4 other friends, mostly local area ladies, who would be bridesmaids, so within a month most details were loosely set in place.

Now it was time for Lisa and Joe to discuss at length the honeymoon plans and they decided to spend it in the Florida Keys. They had decided to rent a house in the Marathon area which was about half way down the Keys, toward Key West, and spend a few days there and to then move on down to Key West where they could stay at any number of locations and simply take in all the historic sites and make a 7-10 day hone moon vacation out of it. They would probably land in Miami and spend a day or two in Key Largo then move gradually down the keys toward Key West. What could be more romantic than a young, just married couple leisurely cruising the Florida keys? What a honeymoon this would be.

You might be surprised at how fast 8 weeks can go by when you're planning for a huge event like the wedding of your lifetime. But before they realized, it was one week before the wedding and Lisa was scrambling to get things lined up. Don't take that wrong though, she was one cool head and that was one of the things Joe cherished most about her. No matter the situation she was always the cool head and was the adult in the room; just a chip off the old block , like her Dad. They even had to rent a full sized organ because the Hilton didn't have one at the time. Lisa's Aunt Lillian was a great pianist and organ player and would serve that function. Lisa's daughter, Lee Ann, age four, would be the flower girl and the ring bearer would be one of Lisa's friend's son, who was four years old as well.

Finally, about a week before the wedding, the details had all come together and all that was left were the bride's shower, the groom's party and the rehearsal dinner the night before the wedding and the reception after the wedding.

Well now all was set. The bride's shower was attended by 52 young women and the bride received numerous gifts that were a nice start for a new marriage. All of the bridesmaids were in attendance including the maid of honor, Phyllis, and the four other bridesmaids, Connie, Loraine, Beth and Judy.

Then there was groom's bachelor party which was hosted by best man, Bern, and the four groomsmen, Jack, Cody, Larry and John. They had their main party downtown at the piano bar and really livened up the place. Joe spent special time talking about the Bay of Pigs invasion of Cuba with his three compadres from the invasion and how they all suffered from anxiety and guilt feelings of being the only 4 survivors of the 8 aircraft who went in there, and how they had been betrayed by their President at the last moment. They did not resent that in time of war that their lives were expendable; but that they had been betrayed by their President after the assault on the beach had already begun.

Then the rehearsal dinner the night before the wedding was attended by Lisa's father, Joe's mother and younger brother Jack, and all the wedding party. Joe's father did not attend due to business conflicts. But the rehearsal went off well, as planned, without a hitch. Both Lisa's father and Joe's mom spoke and related to what an exciting time it was and expressed their happiness that Lisa and Joe were marrying at the right time and place for both.

The next day, September 15th, was their wedding day and it went off perfectly as planned. Bern was there to present the groom and Lisa's Dad walked her down the aisle and Lisa's Dad's whole law firm was present to celebrate the new marriage. No one would ever behold a more beautiful ceremony. And following the ceremony, a reception was held in the dining area of the hotel where there was music with a live band and dancing that featured the bride and her Dad leading things off. A grand time was had by all and the pressure was off now that the grand event was over. Following the reception Lisa and Joe were taken by limousine to the Great Falls Airport, where they boarded the waiting twin Cessna for the trip to the Dallas-Fort Worth airport.

Chapter 2
The Honeymoon

LISA'S DAD HAD A CORPORATE aircraft and had planned to fly the couple to Dallas where they had connections for their flight to Miami. Once there they would rent a car and make a tour of the Florida Keys beginning at Islamorada, FL. Why Islamorada? Because that is the capital of big game fishing. They wanted to catch a sailfish or a big marlin. Then as they went on down the chain they would do whatever came to mind at the moment.

Once on the ground in Miami they were dead tired from the long day and trip and they had a reservation at the nearest hotel, so they slept most of the rest of the day. The following morning they took their car rental and headed for Islamorada, FL. As they were going through the Key Largo area, Lisa exclaimed, "Oh Joe, I never thought I would ever look to the left and see the Atlantic Ocean and then look immediately to the right and see the Gulf of Mexico. What an absolutely spectacular sight to see!" Joe looked and saw it for himself and then suddenly pulled over to the side of the road and said, "We must have a picture of this. This is exactly why I bought that super wide angle lens for my new Nikon camera, the one I bought while I was TDY (temporary duty) to Guam the last time I was there. After Joe had shot several pictures, they got back in the vehicle and resumed their drive to Islamorada. Joe said "When we tell our children about this experience we can back it up with pictures of the occasion." Lisa smiled and said, "Yes, it's true, we can!"

They arrived at their destination about 3:30 that afternoon. They decided they should drive down to the docks and view the fishing boats as they came in from their fishing trips so that they might see the boats with their catches of the day. As they walked the pier they saw the results of the day and decided they would make their reservations for a fishing trip tomorrow. They did so with Capt. Dave Farmer who seemed most knowledgeable and available for a fishing trip the next morning. They would leave the dock at 8 am so they were told to be there about 7:30 am.

The next morning, Joe and Lisa arrived at the dock at 7:30 as requested by the captain and Captain Dave and his crew were already there readying the boat with supplies for the trip. Within 15 minutes of leaving the dock they were putting out their lines and trolling for the big catch. Joe and Lisa were seated in their chairs and ready. They trolled up and down the area for about 30 minutes without a strike so Capt. Dave moved on to another area close by where they continued trolling. About an hour after they had left the dock, Joe got a strike and the fight was on. He thought, and so did Capt. Dave, that it was a medium sized fish, maybe 40 or 50 pounds judging by the weight of the pull on the rod. Joe was strapped in his seat. He reeled the fish in a little at a time not wanting to break the line. Finally after about 5 minutes he had the fish alongside the boat so the captain's mate, Tom, was able to get the net under the fish and pull it into the boat. It was a King Mackerel. The fish weighed out at 42 pounds. Joe and Lisa were now excited and ready to catch more. They continued to troll and kept moving to different spots until finally Lisa had a strike on her line and this one didn't wait to put on a show. It was a huge sailfish that lepted from the water putting up a big fight and each time the fish headed towards the boat Lisa reeled in the slack to keep the line taunt. This one was a wear-you-out type fish, but Lisa kept reeling it in a little at a time each time the fish turned at an angle towards the boat. Finally after about 10 minutes the fish began to tire and as it did she reeled it closer until finally Tom was able to reach the fish and drag it aboard. It tipped the scales at 73 pounds. "Nice catch," said the Captain. They continued trolling the waters in this area. Captain Dave said this was a good fishing spot by his experience. It was about another 45 minutes before there was another strike and this time it was on Joe's line. It was a hard pull and both Joe and Captain Dave knew this was a large fish because not only did it bend the rod a great deal, but it had the effect of moving the transom of the boat. The fight was on and that huge fish gave no ground. The fish was about 125 yards behind the boat when it came out of the water and it was a huge marlin, probably weighing at least 200 pounds. The fight went on for about 15 minutes before that fish ran straight at the boat for a moment and before Joe could even reel in the slack the fish bolted the other direction and broke the line. "Wow, what a fish that was!" exclaimed Joe as he reeled his empty line in.

Tom, the captain's mate baited Joe's line once again and they were back to fishing. Meanwhile, Captain Dave kept switching fishing holes looking for better fishing. A few minutes later Joe had another strike. This time it was another large fish, a marlin that immediately leapt out of the water. The fish looked to be at least 150 lbs. in size. After about 10 minutes of fight they had it alongside the boat so Tom could bring it into the boat. Turned out it weighed out at 174 pounds. About 45 minutes later Lisa got another strike and again you could see it was a nice fish as it came out of the water. She had her hands full, that's for sure. Another good fight ensued for about 12 minutes and when Tom pulled the fish in the boat it was a 147 pound marlin. By now it was 3:30 pm and time to head for the pier.

Photo by permission of Daniel Carney

IT HAD BEEN A GREAT day of fishing and everyone was tired. As they returned to the dock there was the usual crowd waiting to see the day's catch. Liza and Joe had brought their cameras with them so the great day of fishing was preserved forever on film. As they departed they thanked Capt. Dave and Tom for the wonderful outing.

Joe and Lisa got into their vehicle and headed towards Marathon which was about 30 miles down the road. And they couldn't help but talk about what a wonderful day they had. Now the next thing on their agenda was to go scuba diving at Marathon. It had been a beautiful September day with the temperature no higher than 80 degrees. As soon as they arrived at Marathon they checked in at the hotel and located the Scuba diving shop. They already knew that their checkout for scuba diving would involve a short school session in the morning to instruct them on how to use the diving equipment properly and that since neither of them had ever done this before they would need to dive with an instructor with them for the whole dive. They were told by the diving shop that their instructor would go into the swimming pool with them for instruction before going out to the reef on board the diving boat. With all this information in hand they went to their room and prepared for dinner

They decided to eat at the hotel restaurant. As they entered the restaurant they notice they had a combo playing. They were pretty tired after a long fishing trip so they did want to turn in early and get plenty of rest. They both ordered seafood. Lisa ordered boiled shrimp and Joe ordered broiled flounder. The food they graded as delicious; they danced a few hot licks and off to bed they went. They had to be at the pool which was just across the street, at 8:00 am for their scuba diving instruction. When they fell asleep in each other's arms they were still talking about the fun fishing tour they had taken. The last thing Lisa said before going to sleep was, "I always have such a great time when we are together." To which Joe replied, "And you know that is mutual. I have never known anyone else with whom I need no defense shield."

The hotel rang their number at 6:30 am just as instructed. They were up and ready for breakfast by 7:00. They went to the restaurant, ate a good breakfast and headed back to the room to change into their swimsuits. Lisa decided to wear her new almost disgraceful bikini, a new look in bathing suits that many might think disclosed too much. The older generation just didn't know what to make of younger people flaunting their body parts about. Lisa thought it was okay considering they were off down in Florida on vacation. And Joe thought it was okay because he had the best looking woman around and he relished seeing other guys with those mouth watering looks at her.

After having their orientation in the pool they were to report to the scuba diving boat at 1:00 pm where they met their instructor again. They were among about 10 divers who were at various stages of their diving experiences. Some of them were at the stage where they could go solo without an instructor, while others like Joe and Lisa were having a new experience. They went out about 2 miles to a coral reef area where the boat stopped and anchored. Then they all did their preparation of checking their equipment, Joe and Lisa being under direct supervision of their instructor.

Soon Joe, Lisa and their instructor entered the water, put on their weighted belts and began their dive down to 30 ft. The three of them explored the coral reef and viewed all the beautiful living sea fish and underwater wonders that they had only previously seen in pictures. They did see a few sand sharks but none of them showed any interest in them. It was as if all these wonderful creatures of the deep were in complete harmony; all just cohabitating the ecosystem of the underworld that only these creatures understand. Fortunately they had been able to procure an underwater camera so that some of these memories could be preserved for posterity.

Pixabay.com free images

AND ALL TOO SOON THEY were at the end of their time, for it was time to surface. So the three of them, Lisa, Joe and their instructor surfaced and were back in the boat and headed back to the dock. "What a wonderful experience," Lisa said. "I can't wait to see the underwater pictures you took Joe."

When they got back to the dock Joe and Lisa thanked their instructor for a wonderful trip, tipped him and they were off to their hotel room. Joe and Lisa decided that they would cancel the rental house at Marathon because they really wanted to spend more time in Key West and hoped to meet people who had known Earnest Hemingway, who had, on July 2ndof that very year, committed suicide at his home in Ketchum, Idaho. Joe himself had thought for a long time that he too might like to be a writer. Joe's mother had written several short stories. She, he told Lisa, loved to write fictional short stories. "I just wish I had her powers of imagination. She can really think up a story," he said. So to find out as much as he could about the life and times of Earnest Hemingway was of vast importance to Joe. He really wanted to know what made this guy tick.

They stayed for another night in Marathon. They noticed that the people in there seemed to have their own laid back attitude about life and the government. While they were sitting in the hotel bar that evening they were having a conversation with the bartender. According to the bartender, one of the main reasons he lived in the Keys was that the people there felt that they were an independent part of the United States. He said they didn't want advice or money from the U.S. government and they didn't want to give them any either. They liked their simple life and just wanted the government to leave them alone. Joe and Lisa were now 'in stitches' and literally bent over laughing. Joe said, "That's exactly the way we feel. You know there aren't enough of us left who feel that way since Roosevelt introduced us to Socialism in the 1930s." They then rose and did some hot licks on the dance floor and

Joe showed Lisa a new dance called the "Bop" and some new moves on the Jitterbug, which some might call the East Coast Swing.

Joe and Lisa returned to their room and spent some time talking about their day before going off to sleep. This was just sort of an unwritten law between them. They never liked to sleep until they had sorted through the day's events. Joe had never had this with any other woman and this was what was so different about their relationship. Joe never felt threatened by her, nor she by him. So it was like everyday was a new experience between two people who truly worshipped the ground the other walked on. Occasionally they might see things a little differently, but by the time they finished talking they were both on the same page.

The next morning Joe and Lisa slept in until about 9:30 am. They awakened in no hurry to leave and packed up for the trip further south to Key West. They had their breakfast in the restaurant and then loaded the car for departure. They had brochures of the Keys, including the area they were about to cross, which was called 7 Mile Bridge. According to history this bridge had been constructed between 1909 and 1912 by a couple of railroad tycoons, Henry Flagler and Clarence S. Coe, as an extension of the railroad past Marathon and into the southern Keys. It connected Knight's Key with Pigeon Key by way of Moser Channel and Pacet Channel. Needless to say, crossing a bridge this long was simply an awesome experience. They continued driving until they finally saw the U.S. Navel Base where Joe had been taken for emergency care after his rescue from the waters just south of Cuba earlier that year; though he still had no recollection of any of the crash.

Joe and Lisa wanted a hotel room as close as possible to Duvall street because that was where they thought most of the activity would be. They found one and then set out on foot to see what they could see before dark. It was now about 5:30 pm so they would find a place to eat while they were downtown. They knew they wanted to find Sloppy Joe's Bar because they wanted to try for an audience with friends of the great novel writer himself, Earnest Hemingway. They hoped they would just happen to be there at the right time.

Author photo

THEY DID FIND SLOPPY Jo's bar and did ask about Hemingway. Different people with whom they spoke gave slightly different accounts, but most of the reports were that Hemingway was an affable kind of guy with different moods depending on when you saw him. There also were many quotes that had been attributed to him and they all illustrated his deep philosophical nature.

The sunsets at Key West were legendary and Joe and Lisa wanted to experience those for themselves so they went searching for and found Mallory Square. Joe said, "Look, you can see the changing colors of the rainbow at the end of the day. It's like passing from an old world into a new one as the colors of the sky change. Today is gone and now we wait for the dawning of a new day tomorrow."

Author photo

THE NEXT MORNING THEY went to see the farthest point south of the United States. The folks in Key West label themselves as being from The Conch Republic, for just as the bartender at Marathon had told them, they really wanted nothing to do with the U.S. government. Lisa took Joe's picture at the Southernmost Point in the Continental U.S.A, Key West, FL.

Author photo

AFTER TAKING MORE PICTURES, they walked the beach. They walked barefoot along the beach just in the edge of the water. The sand was soft and squished through their toes, the tide was going out, the water was a deep green in color. Other people were out walking the beaches as well. The waves seemed calmer than in the evening. They also made plans for a sailboat ride the next day.

Author photo

THEN THEY MADE IT BACK to Sloppy Joe's for a few drinks and another visit with more people who knew the famous author, Hemingway. Since it had been only two months since his death, it seemed that most conversation at Sloppy Joe's was about him.

Hemingway had bought the home in Key West in 1931 and had live there through 1939. After that he bought a home in Cuba about 10 miles southeast of Havana where he had spent most of his time until 1960 when he moved to Ketchum, Idaho. He was a cordial friend of Fidel Castro and was his supporter, but he also had 'varied feelings' about his politics. General Batista had ruled by Military Junta for years before Castro finally overthrew his dictatorship, vowing to do right by the people of Cuba. But instead he introduced them to communism and their living standards became some of the lowest in the world. Joe told Lisa that the result of the Castro takeover was the exact reason for the Bay of Pigs invasion. Joe was angry at President John Kennedy and he still felt the invasion was justified based on the cards that Castro was already playing. His only regret was the loss of his flying buddies and the ones on the ground whom they were trying to help. With that Joe said, "Enough on that for now. We can get back to more pleasant thoughts."

"The world breaks everyone, and afterward,
some are strong at the broken places."

Earnest Hemingway

Joe called this quote to Lisa's attention and said, "I don't think that truer words were spoken than those." "You are exactly right," said Lisa.

The following day they arrived at the boat dock and their boat captain was ready to take them sailing to view the local area. He used the boat engine to get the boat headed out to sea and then he raised the sails. There was about a 10 knot breeze blowing and it made for good sailing and also made it cool for them. They sailed up and down the coast for a couple of hours, the water was a beautiful deep green color and there were just enough waves to make the boat oscillate up and down enough to create a fine spray that hit them in the face as they stood on the boat. There were several dolphins running alongside the boat and all this made the time on the water a magnificent experience. After 2 hours they arrived back at the dock having had a very wonderful and relaxing orientation ride around the area.

The final thing they wanted to do before leaving Key West was to walk the grounds at Hemingway's house, so they thought it would not hurt to ask. To their surprise the housekeeper was there and graciously allowed them to visit the grounds.

Author photo

THEY SAW THE 6 AND 7 toed cats, the house, the pool

Author photo

AND THE SMALL QUARTERS out back where upstairs Hemingway did his writing.

Author photo

AND THE TYPEWRITER that he had used to write was still sitting on the desk just where he used it. The house keeper said he usually wrote only about 500 words a day and then he would go to Sloppy Joe's if he didn't go fishing for Marlin that day. This was the highlight of their visit. It made the whole trip worth the time and effort it took to come. They were also told that Hemingway's father-in-law had bought the house for him and his wife, as a wedding gift, for $8000 in 1931 and they lived there until 1939. During that period Hemingway's wife had put in the pool and had a tall fence put around the property. It is said to be the first house in Key West to have inside plumbing. However, Hemingway decided in 1940 that he wanted to move to Cuba. Why? Was it that the marlin fishing was better there or that he had a special love for the Spanish people? But then Hemingway was a very complex person. Why was he such a great writer?

Joe was so excited. He felt that this adventure to the property of Ernest Hemingway was the highlight of their honeymoon trip. Joe knew Hemingway was an avid sports fisherman, but why was he such a great writer? There is no certainty as to why he went to Cuba unless he did, indeed, think that it was better fishing for marlin, one of, if not the greatest, sporting fish there ever was or has been. Anyway, in 1940 he purchased a house about 10 miles southeast of Havana where he would live and write for the rest of his professional life. He paid $12,500 for the property and it had 13 acres of banana trees. He would live there until 1960. His fishing boat, the Pilar, was left there on the beach in 1960 when he moved to Ketchum, Idaho. Even though he was good friends with Castro, Hemingway is said to have said that the revolution was an *historical necessity*. But his personal feelings about the man, Fidel Castro were varied. However, Joe believed Hemingway was extremely disappointed in the changes Castro made after wrestling control of the island country from the Military Junta of General Batista.

Later in life, Joe would see that Hemingway's ultimate undoing was major mental depression, which was poorly understood at that time at best. It has also been said that alcoholism was involved; but if one understands much on this subject, one would understand that what people with major depression frequently do is try to treat their depression with alcohol. Alcohol has the immediate effect of creating a momentary high but unfortunately that high is followed by slam dunk depression. There were few medicines for treating depression at that time. The tricyclic antidepressants were just coming out, the main one being Elavil, and that drug had about as many negative effects as it did positive effects, so it was not well taken by most patients and generally that left only one option and that was electroshock therapy, which Hemingway had twice at the Mayo Clinic in Rochester, Minnesota. Hemingway went home from his second treatment and killed himself two days later. What a shame, with the medications soon to be available he might have been saved and might have written many more great books.

Young Joe had been curious all of his life about what was different between great men and the run of the mill, average man. As another example, he wondered why the U.S. General feared most by the Germans was George S. Patten and not Eisenhower?

But Joe put away his thoughts and he and Lisa decided they had seen enough of the Keys and were ready to head back north to Miami. Lisa said, "Why don't we change our itinerary and stop by old New Orleans on the way back home to Montana?" Joe said, "That's a wonderful idea. As soon as we get to the hotel room or if we see a pay phone we can do that." It was almost sundown and time to go watch the sunset. They made it to the beach just in time for the sunset and it was gorgeous as usual. The sky was clear but with a few clouds far out. They watched the clouds and the sky change colors as the sunset slowly began. And the brilliant sun dropped slowly further down behind the bluish pink skies and the skies changed colors as though there was magic in the air. A more beautiful majestic change of colors they had never seen. Joe said, "I guess you might say a Key West sunset has all the colors of the rainbow and that's why they are so beautiful. No wonder people say you haven't seen a beautiful sunset until you have seen the sunset at Key West."

After Joe and Lisa made their change of reservations with the airlines to include a stop in old New Orleans, they got their showers and snuggled up and talked about the wonderful trip they had had so far. Just like two young lovers they went to sleep cuddled in each other's arms.

The morning came early, around 6:00, so they would still have time to make an early breakfast and get on the road. They had to fly out of Miami at 5:45 pm and arrive in New Orleans at about 8:20 pm. They had reservations at the New Orleans Hotel for that night. They had made their plans for two days in New Orleans and the return flight to Great Falls by way of Dallas-Fort Worth.

They arrived in Miami and their flight was on time all the way to New Orleans. Once they arrived at the New Orleans Hotel they unloaded their baggage and headed just across Canal Street to Bourbon Street. Joe had been here many times before, but it was all new to Lisa. Her eyes were as big as saucers. She didn't know quite what to think. She was dressed in tight green pants and blouse, which made her emerald eyes more pronounced. To Joe she was beautiful any way she dressed. And he was dressed in jeans and an open collared sport shirt.

Author photo

ONCE ON BOURBON STREET they walked slowly, taking in all the sights before deciding where to eat. They finally stopped at the

Court of Two Sisters Restaurant, went in and were seated. This was Lisa's first taste of real New Orleans French Cuisine and she was delighted. After dinner they went strolling over to the renowned Pat O'Brian's Bar and had a few drinks. Joe had told Lisa about the famous Hurricane drink and how easy it was to get extremely drunk on them almost before you realized it. They saw some really strange looking people walking the streets. Then there were the shoeshine boys snapping their cloths on the streets and also the tap dancers and street musicians who would be grateful if you dropped some change into their bucket. Joe said to Lisa, "This is the home of blues music, as I'm sure you can tell."

Author photo

TOMORROW THEY WOULD do some daytime walking to see the sights and then that night they were heading home to Montana. The next morning found Joe and Lisa visiting such sights as the Jackson

Cathedral and the River Walk and some of the shops, as well as the old train station to sample those famous Cajun Benet's and chicory coffee.

Chapter 3
Off to School

LISA AND JOE ARRIVED back in Great Falls in late September. They had talked a great deal about their future while on their honeymoon and now they were together in their thinking. They were both committed to Joe going to medical school; it was just a matter of determining the details. The only problem at this point, as Joe saw it, was where he should do his training. Lisa said that Montana had no medical school, so they would need to move. Joe said, "Mississippi has a four year medical school and I can also fly with the Air National Guard which will be extra pay and I can draw the GI Bill and that will help pay our expenses. And while I am going to school you could go ahead and get your law degree as well from Ole Miss. That way we could both be getting our educations in our respective fields and see what works out from there." And so it was decided.

The first thing they wanted to do was thank and hug her Dad for the wonderful wedding for which he had been the principal provider. They wanted to put Lisa's Dad in the loop about their plans, as well to see what his wise council might suggest about them. So they had dinner with her Dad the next night and discussed the plans they were kicking around. Her Dad listened with care and said, "That all sounds like a reasonable plan and if the two of you need support from me, you know I am more than willing to help you." Joe said, "Well, you know that I will need to finish up with my pre med degree first, but if I go to school year round I can probably do it in about 2 years. That means that I could finish my B.S. degree in about 2 years, considering I would get some college credits for my past military training, and that probably means that I could be in medical school in 1964 or 1965. And, Lisa could commute to Ole Miss and get her law degree while I'm finishing up my pre-med degree. The details can be worked out later but I think our overall plan is a reasonable one."

Lisa's Dad then asked, "What about Lee Ann? You will need to decide where she will live." Lisa immediately said, "We've discussed her too. Hopefully Aunt Lillian will not mind keeping her for a bit longer while we get settled in Mississippi and then I'll fly back and take her to live with us in Starkville." Her Dad finally smiled and said, "Sounds like you two will be very busy for the next few years." Lisa kissed her Dad good night, Joe gave him a hug and they left for Lisa's house.

Once they were home and in bed Joe said, "I feel much better knowing we have your Dad's support." "Yes," said Lisa, "he has never been stingy where I'm concerned. He has always been the kind of Dad who gives me room to grow on my own, but who has always been there for me if I stub my toe. He has never tried to smother me, yet when I've made errors he has always been there for me in a healthy kind of way. I don't think I could have a better Dad." "I agree," said Joe.

So Joe and Lisa made their way to Starkville, MS and were able to find space in the student housing. The housing was old WW2 barracks that had been converted into student housing. They were located just across the road from the Poultry Department of Mississippi State University. They were two-storied apartments and they came in one, two, or three bedroom versions. There was no air conditioning and there was one big gas heater in the living room. You really did not have to sweep the trash very far across the floor because it would just sift through the cracks of the wooden planked floor. There were about 300 units and the size unit you got depended on how many children you had. It was for married students only. No singles. The single students all lived in dorms or out in town if they could afford to do so.

Those who lived in the "tar paper shacks" as the married students called them, thought they were quite adequate and the rent was cheap, $25 dollars a month, and the gas bill was split up among the dwellers which came to about $25 dollars but only during the winter months. You knew it was cold when the dog's water on the kitchen floor had ice in it the next morning. If you had a little help from home you were allowed to put in a window air conditioner unit, but you had to pay your own electric bill. So for about $50 per month you, your wife and kids had a place to live. It was a poor living but everyone else was poor as well, so Joe and Lisa accepted the situation as just part of the cost of an education. Most of the students had part-time jobs, as did their wives, and they were all happy to sacrifice now for greater things in the future. There was very little free time and that was to go to a football or basketball game, but student tickets were only about 6 or 7 dollars. Unhappy? Heavens no, they didn't have time to be unhappy. Campus life was quiet and students were either at home studying or at the library.

Mississippi Air Guard

N ow young Joe Ruff took a full academic load and also commuted to Meridian, MS three weekends a month to fly with the Air National Guard. Flying with the Air Guard was not easy because the Air Guard had to fill all the squares and requirements that the regular Air Force did. It was hard, but everyone was in the same boat and you just did what you had to and didn't sleep much. Joe's grandfather still ran a dairy farm, the Sunflower Dairy, at that time; so on the weekends that Joe went to Meridian he would take an ice chest and three one gallon big mouth jugs and fill them with milk from his grandfather's dairy and the cost savings on the milk just about paid the gas bill for the small Volvo car.

Author family photo

THAT LITTLE VOLVO ALONG, with an old air cooled bug (VW), made it so they kept their living expenses low. They saved every penny.

Gasoline was 20 to 25 cents a gallon. If it sounds like they were poor then yes, they were, but they had lots of company. Even though they could ask for and receive help from Lisa's Dad, they declined to do so. Beyond being full time students and part time workers, they had little time for other things. Joe's Air National Guard pay for flying on weekends was about $150 dollars a month and his GI bill was $160 dollars a month, so they were able to get along alright for being both in college and law school at the same time. Joe and Lisa were looking forward, not backward, and they were willing to do whatever it took to achieve their goals.

It was at this point that Joe and Lisa realized that with Joe studying and flying and Lisa commuting to Ole Miss for her classes every day, which was quite a drive, that time for little Lee Ann was going to be very sparse. They called and talked with Aunt Lillian and with Lee Ann to see if it would be too terribly inconvenient for Aunt Lillian to keep Lee Ann a bit longer until they could see their way clear to bring her to Mississippi. And she gladly agreed. She loved Lee Ann as her own child and Lee Ann was very happy to stay with her Aunt.

Joe had not flown now for nearly a year. In fact, the flight during which he was shot down was his last flight. His self-confidence was low about this time. He asked himself, "Can I still fly a high performance aircraft or am I now afraid of flying?" This was the demon he was battling now. The Air Guard decided to put Joe on active duty for the period of his checkout in the T33 and following that for a period of as long as necessary to checkout in the RF84F, commonly called by the pilots "the Hog" because of its excessively long take off rolls. It was common for the Hog to use as much as 6500 feet of runway before liftoff at 155 knots on an 8000 foot runway. Joe was used to that in the B47 though. He was more worried about his overall confidence level since being shot down in the Bay of Pigs invasion.

So right after New Year's 1962, Joe had his first ride in the back seat of the T33, an instrument ride under the hood. Joe was very critical of himself after that first instrument flight, but the pilot in the front seat insisted he did very well. Joe's instrument flying at that time did not meet the criteria he had set for himself. He did push ahead and finish his checkout in the T33. You see, a checkout in the T33 was necessary so that flight operations could see whether you could fly well enough to move on to the RF84F training. Remember, the RF84F was a single seater so you only had a chase pilot behind you to advise you if needed. He couldn't take the controls and land the aircraft, so you had better get it right. Joe's transition into the RF84F went smoothly.

However, on his first night flight in the local area on a Friday night, Joe took off in a formation flight of two with the real hotshot pilot of the unit, K.B. Shirley. Shirley promptly climbed the two of them to 20,000 feet while getting clearance from Meridian approach control because they were now entering the clouds. This was a new experience for Joe, flying close wing formation while in the clouds. You're talking about vertigo? You got it right, most pilots would have refused to fly close wing tip formation in the clouds, but not Joe. He hung in there until K.B. decided he had punished the new recruit enough. Finally, they did an instrument penetration approach from 20,000 feet and Joe was congratulated on a good ride.

Also during Joe's checkout on his first photo mission, his first target was a bridge near the town of Jackson, Alabama. He was to pop down on the target from a higher altitude and shoot a forward picture. Just after shooting the picture at 500 feet altitude, he scanned his engine instruments, as a pilot is supposed to, and noticed that his engine oil pressure had dropped from 20 pounds to 4 pounds, which was not a good thing. It was below the red line. He was about 50 miles from home. He called Key tower while slowly climbing. He was afraid to add any power for fear of aggravating a bad situation. The oil pressure lubricates the bearings of the turbine. So while he was heading back to the base the rescue fire group was notified and raced to the approach end of Runway 35. When Joe got to 3 miles out he lowered the gear and at the appropriate time dropped full flaps and landed. Maintenance took the airplane straight to the hanger and pulled the engine out and when they did the engine bearings fell all over the floor. Joe had dodged another bullet. What was this, an Angel or something?

After much more training by the prescribed book, according to Air Force criteria he was ready for his check ride. The Guard pilots had to meet Air Force Standards. In fact, there was a regular Air Force pilot in town when Joe came due for his check ride to qualify as combat ready. So, the check ride was scheduled with USAF regular Major Robinson from Shaw AFB in South Carolina, which was the Meridian parent wing in the USAF. The whole idea of this check flight was to plan the flight to the assigned targets, brief the check pilot and to execute the flight exactly as briefed. So having done all those things the check pilot would line up behind and in the chase position on the runway and see if you could execute the flight the way you briefed it. All this was done in radio silence using only hand signals. They would climb in formation to high altitude, and then descend rapidly into the target area, shoot the pictures at a specified altitude and then pop back up to high altitude for the trip home, all with radio silence.

So Joe lined up for takeoff with Major Robinson in the chase position. Joe signaled that he was pushing the throttle to 100% and when he received the ready signal from Major Robinson, Joe released his brakes and 10 seconds later Major Robinson released his brakes. After they had both lifted off at 155 knots, the plan was for Major Robinson to cut Joe off in the turnout of traffic which he did. Joe climbed at 98% power in order for Major Robinson to have 2% power to use to stay in proper formation, then Joe leveled off at 90% power. They climbed to the briefed altitude of 20,000 feet and Joe signaled a level off which the other pilot acknowledged by a thumb and nod of the head. When they reached a specified distance from the target area Joe signaled to pull the power back to 85% to begin his descent, they were right on track according to Joe's map.

Joe saw the first target coming up and his alignment was perfect. He turned on his camera and shot that one, a perfect shot. They turned toward the second target and got perfect shots at targets 2, 3, and 4. And it was a good thing they were finished because they were just about at "bingo" fuel level. Joe signaled that he was pushing the throttle up and heading home in a steady climb. Joe pushed his power to 98%. Again, this was to give the chase pilot a 2% edge so that he could keep the formation closed up. There were a bunch of little puff ball clouds that they would have to fly through just ahead. It was a no sweat situation but Joe pointed to the clouds and Major Robinson put a thumbs up. When they hit the clouds there was a bit of turbulence and at that moment Joe's left external fuel tank jettisoned itself from the aircraft. Major Robinson was far enough out that the tank was not a hazard to him. Joe immediately called Key tower and told the tower operator that he had lost his left external fuel tank near Oxford, Mississippi. He was not declaring an emergency because they had plenty of fuel, but he didn't know about injuries on the ground.

The fact is that the fuel tank landed in the middle of a colored man's cow pasture. The Air Guard sent a delegation the next day to settle the account. The only damage was a small crater in the ground about 2 feet deep. The Air Guard took the remains of the tank and filled in the crater it had left in the ground. Just as the Air Guard envoy was about to depart, the elderly colored gentleman who owned the field said, "What about some money?" The officer in charge said, "There does not appear to be any damage sir." To which the colored gentleman replied, "Well sir, I think I ought to get a little somethin' for being scared."

Joe led the formation of two back to Meridian and landed at Key Field without further incident. Joe admitted to himself that he had put his best foot forward on this check ride so he felt good about the flight. His instructor chase pilot felt stronger about it than that. He told J.B. Parsons, Jr., who had done much of the teaching of 1st Lt. Joe Ruff, "I didn't know the Air Force still trained pilots that well.' Joe got high marks on his check ride because of the great instruction from instructor pilots in the 163rd Tactical Reconnaissance Squadron. They were not slackers. They were all good at what they were doing and cared deeply about their mission. AND, they were all patriots.

Class 62D, Air National Guard Instrument School

The next stop for Lt. Ruff was the Air National Guard Jet Instrument School, a one month school at Ellington AFB in Houston, Texas. Lt. Joe was lucky to get the best instructor in the whole bunch. His name was Poncho Via to his friends. Lt. Joe thought he knew how to fly instruments when he got there but there was another whole awakening when he crawled in the back seat of that T33, or T-bird as it was referred to by the pilots, with Poncho Via in the front seat. Poncho taught him things about instrument flying that young Joe would never have otherwise known.

The flight always began with Poncho lining the T-bird up with the center of the runway with Joe already under the hood and running the engine up to 100% power and then saying, "You have the aircraft." What Joe then had to do was keep it heading straight down the runway, using the brakes until the aircraft gained enough speed to steer it with the rudder and once clearly airborne asking the instructor to raise the gear and then the flaps making what amounted to a zero outside visibility takeoff. Try that one on for size. Sound easy to you? The secret was to hold the exact heading, no tolerance through lift off, gear up, flaps up and climb. And that was only the beginning. Then there was partial panel flying with just the needle and ball without the attitude indicator while bouncing around through the clouds. Joe thought he was a good instrument pilot until he got with Poncho Via, but he had never even scratched the surface. Poncho was an amazing pilot and teacher and Joe would never forget him.

Now you need to know that this was not a required school. It was strictly voluntary. And you knew who the pilots were who had attended that school. If the weather was bad or marginal for the mission, you know who they would send to fly that mission. Not everyone was a natural or gifted instrument pilot. They, as in any other line of work, come in all sizes and varieties. Everyone has had vertigo at one time or another, even great instrument pilots. The key is this: If you feel like you are upside down but your instruments say otherwise, a good instrument pilot believes what his instruments tell him every time and makes his moves of the controls and trim accordingly. And that is the difference between a great instrument pilot and a pilot that's getting ready to have an airplane wreck, or as some would say a train wreck. If not being able to see the horizon bothers you and you are a pilot, then maybe you should find another line of work.

The F84F and the RF84F were built by Republic Aircraft. They were heavy airplanes and used a lot of runway to get off the ground but once airborne they were sweet flying machines. They were also durable and a pilot like Joe could fly through a man-eater of a thunderstorm and know that the airplane was not going to break apart on him. There have even been isolated cases of an F84F taking out the top of a pine tree and landing safely. Don't believe it? Ask any guy who flew F84s. If there was a negative to the Air National Guard instrument school, it would be that the RF84F pilot knew he could fly through anything and his aircraft was not going to break up on him. Only thing was, when you saw a big thunderstorm coming up ahead, be sure to pull your seatbelt down nice and snug and lower the seat all the way down. Otherwise your helmet was going to be bouncing off that canopy and that didn't feel so good. Once you got yourself snugged down, when you hit the turbulence just let the thing go, hang on, don't fight it. It might shoot you down 3 or 4 thousand feet, then the next updraft will probably take you back up by that much. Just tell Traffic Control Center to hang on, you'll be back with them as soon as you get through this thing. You see, the whole thing was about not fighting the aircraft, just hang with that attitude indicator and manage the attitude of the aircraft. Then in a minute or so that bastard thunderstorm would spit you out the other side. And think how proud you were of that "Hog" you were driving. That's the kind of confidence the Air Guard Instrument School inspired in the students who went through that program. And that was what Lt. Ruff told his operations officer, Major "Sore Butt" as he was fondly called behind his back. The truth was though that the Major had his hands full with Joe and a couple of his Musketeer buddies. There were three, you might say, who were bad asses, but all three were great pilots, the kind you would want to have on your wing in combat.

The RF84F was equipped for air to ground gunnery and the Squadron had that square to fill as well. They shot air to ground gunnery at Camp Shelby near Hattiesburg, Mississippi several times each year. They also participated in an exercise at Fort Campbell Army Base and Joe got credit for killing the Regiment Commander. Well, my goodness, there he was standing right by his Jeep on Joe's gunnery pass. What did he expect?

Back to School for Joe & Lisa

In the meantime, Lisa was hard at work on her degree in law at Ole Miss while Joe was carrying a full student load at Mississippi State University. She commuted daily to Oxford, which was about an hour's drive each way. A hardship, yes, but they were both young and were able to do it even though it left them little time together. They both knew it was a hard row to hoe when they started but it wouldn't be forever. Joe's Air Guard participation took 3 weekends per month so they savored that one weekend per month they had together like it was gold plated. On the alternate weekends, Lisa would sometimes fly to Great Falls to be with Lee Ann or her Dad would fly down with Lee Ann. He was truly a wonderful father and made it as easy as he could for all concerned. Joe had always heard from the older folks that it was amazing how much good work young people could do when they put their minds to it. And probably that's why God gave children to young people.

While Joe was at Mississippi State University he knew that he needed to make the Straight A honor roll in order to get into medical school because of that straight C honor roll he had made his first year in college at LSU. By his calculations, he thought if he made nothing less than a B he would have a shot at getting in, but he really needed mostly A's with maybe a few B's. But C grades were a non starter. He took a speech class that 1st year and he made all A's on the first 6 speeches he gave. Things were going well, but then he gave a speech on the 'Bay of Pigs Invasion of Cuba' and how President Kennedy had promised air cover for the B26s who were the air support for the ground invasion, and how Kennedy had reneged on his promise when he had 2 aircraft carriers sitting just 2 miles off the Cuban coast. And Joe told no one that he was one of the four of eight B26s who were shot down.

A very young man was teaching this class. Joe got a grade of C on that speech and that was followed by a C on the next two speeches. It was obvious that this man was punishing Joe for his Bay of Pigs speech and that teacher was a Kennedy supporter. Finally, the teacher had to be out of town one week and a lady teacher subbed for him. Joe gave a speech that day and got a grade of A. With this Joe went to see the Dean of Men about the matter and from then on Joe got all A's on the rest of his speeches and an A for the course.

Joe was an arch conservative and had been all of his life. Generally the apple doesn't fall far from the tree. His father was of the same persuasion. And unfortunately, or fortunately, this curse would follow him for the rest of his life. And if anyone asked his opinion he was always a straight shooter with what he thought. He was always willing to listen, but once he had listened to the other side's argument, he then made his judgement call and he stuck to his guns. He was not bashful about letting people know what his thoughts were. Joe was anything but a passive type.

There was a lot of talk about Washington politicians wanting to pass a law for medical care for the elderly. Joe said he would much prefer to take what the patient could pay for the bill, be that in money, pigs or chickens. And if they were penniless, he would rather treat them for free than have the government involved. He really thought he wanted to be a small town country doctor and he felt that he and the patient could reach an equitable settlement on the bill without the nose of big government being part of the equation. And Joe predicted that once the camel's nose was in the tent it would be all over but the crying of this group or that group.

The tar paper shacks where the married students lived were, for whatever reason, called "Westside." MSU decided that with a massive amount of tax money the school would build new apartments for the married students. One might think that the married students would welcome this development with open arms. Not on your life! The married students were happy where they were and knew what a great deal they already had. Joe, Lisa and most others protested, not carrying signs and marching up and down, but vocally. It was to no avail, the decision was made from above. Old Westside would be torn down and new apartments would be built out on the south side of town, far out of walking distance to class. Joe sarcastically said, "I think they call this progress or something like that." The rent on the new apartments would start at $75 per month.

There was a Ford dealership just down the road, Highway 12, called Templeton Ford. The mother of the Templeton brothers who owned the dealership knew and liked Lisa. She offered to allow Joe and Lisa to live in the old frame house behind the dealership where the older Templeton's had raised their two sons. This was a wonderful idea because by now Joe used a small motor scooter to get back and forth to class, so it was a time and gas saver, and every penny counted.

Joe would never forget when out of the clear blue the older Mrs. Templeton decided that she would have her sons loan Joe one of their new cars off the floor to ride down to Jackson for his medical school interview. Both Joe and Lisa were just awe stricken. Such a nice gesture. Joe took them up on their offer. On the way to Jackson that day, Joe would later remember how hard it was raining on the Natchez Trace. As he was driving along at about 60 mph suddenly the car hit a large collection of water and went into a broad side skid in the middle of the road. The car skidded for about what seemed 100 yards and then hit a drier place and spontaneously recovered all on its own. Joe was terrified, not for his life but for fear of wrecking this new car. It had been a totally undeserved favor on the Templeton's part to loan this new car to Joe for the afternoon. Fortunately no one was traveling the opposite direction at that time or it would have been an awful accident. In some ways it seemed that Joe had led a charmed and protected life. Was it that Angel again?

His mind immediately flashed back a few years to a night flight in the B47 when they were flying over Los Angeles about midnight. It was an especially dark night outside. Joe could see lights on the ground identifying Los Angeles but he could see no stars, just blackness outside the cockpit. Everything was running normally when the aircraft commander in the front seat said, "Joe don't get excited or touch the controls, but put your hands very close to the control yoke. But don't touch it. I have made a big mistake. I forgot to change the fuel selector to the rear tank when I should have and I have used all the fuel out of the forward tank. The aircraft is on autopilot now but should the situation become more out of balance, the autopilot may trip to the off position, and if it does the aircraft may pitch up violently and break the aircraft apart. Right now I have put the fuel selector on the rear tank and if we are lucky we can use fuel out of the rear tank rapidly and correct the situation. Sorry, I just made a bone head error." Joe said, "OK." His hands were close around the control yoke in the rear seat but not touching. The next 10-15 minutes were anxious and the auto pilot did not trip off. About 15 minutes later their center of gravity was back to normal. The fear had been whether with both pilots on the controls, could they keep the aircraft from pitching up violently if the auto pilot tripped off, which they would never know for sure, and that was good. Once again, is there an Angel around?

There was a federal farm research lab just across the highway from Westside where Joe worked in the greenhouse a few times for $1.65 per hour, but he was only an occasional fill in. This was three times as much as most jobs around paid at the time. Joe was fortunate though because with his Air Guard and GI Bill money together they had about $300 dollars a month. But they still had to budget their money carefully and Lisa was an excellent money manager, so Joe left that to her discretion.

Joe also had one friend who was a Civil Engineering student who had no money to attend college. So he worked in the oil fields in the Gulf of Mexico one semester and then attended college at Mississippi State the next semester. Alternating work and school took him twice as long, but he made it and graduated. There were many such cases that Joe knew of. He felt fortunate that he had gone in the military early and was now enjoying the spoils of his prior sacrifices. Joe believed that anyone at the time who really wanted a higher education could find a way to get one. The University itself employed many students, or their wives, part-time.

Mississippi State had always been a boy's only school until in the 1950s when it finally became a co-ed school. Prior to that if you attended State and you needed a date you had to go 30 miles east to Columbus, Mississippi to MSCW, Mississippi State College For Women, to find her.

Between Mississippi State and MSCW there was a little hole-in-the-road restaurant called The Crossroads. It was located at the junction of Highways 82 going east and Highway 45 running north and south. Thus it was called "The Crossroads." There had been a many a beer drunk at The Crossroads during as many years. It was a favorite hangout on the weekends. If you didn't have a date to pick up at the "W," as MSCW was called, and you didn't have studying to do, and you were single, and Joe was not, you hung out at The Crossroads.

And football in those days was a joke at Mississippi State. They just looked like a bunch of good ole boys that had not practiced but just gotten together and suited up to play the game for fun. Ole Miss on the other hand had what was usually a nationally ranked team and they were coached by the coaching legend Johnny Vaught. State might win one out of every five games. But their fans were loyal and it made that 'every 5th year win' just as sweet.

Now in basketball, that was another whole story. The SEC was usually decided between Adolph Rump's Kentucky Wildcats and Babe

McCarthy's Mississippi State Bull Dogs. And most times it was determined by who was the home team for that game. When the Bulldogs played Kentucky they had to play in the renowned Rupp Arena at Kentucky and when the Wildcats came to Starkville they had to play the Bulldogs in that small but packed gym where there was so much noise you couldn't even think let alone hear the person sitting next to you. You just knew each game was a championship game all on its own. That's what MSU and Kentucky basketball was like. Joe and Lisa attended the games and it was great fun to see the Bulldogs play in a game where they competed to win. They were also competitive in baseball since they had a great baseball coach Ron Davis, who was his own man as well. But as for Joe and Lisa, they didn't have much time for leisure because they studied most of the time. Matter of fact, they barely had time to speak.

Each year the Meridian Air Guard did two weeks of active duty at the Gulfport Airport in Gulfport, Mississippi. This was a requirement of all National Guard Units.

Lisa had classes that did not match up with the summer schedule, so she, like most of the wives, went down to Gulfport on the middle weekend of summer camp, and was there to meet Joe as they all returned to Key Field in Meridian from summer camp. In both instances it was one gala celebration.

At that time when Dr. James Ellsworth headed the Zoology Department, Joe was the only one, up to that time, 1964, to ever make a 100% score on both the bones and the muscle anatomy of the cat in his comparative anatomy class. He thus received an invitation to join an honorary academic fraternity. But at the time he had to decline because he didn't have the money for the initiation fee, which was $50.

During his time at Mississippi State Joe only made one C and that was in physical chemistry and he had already heard ahead of time the it was a giant killer. The rumors were right. It was the only course he had taken that seemed insurmountable, but he did manage to make a

C. There were only 5 or 6 in the class and everyone seemed to have a difficult time with it. He had an overall average at Mississippi State of 3.8 and with his bad year at LSU and his grades from the University of Arizona included he still had a 3.5 overall. He interviewed and received his letter of acceptance to the University of Mississippi Medical School on December 23, 1963. Also by this time Lisa had just finished her law degree in Oxford, from the University of Mississippi.

When Joe and the registrar at MSU looked at his credits it was found that if they included all the credits he had earned at LSU, University of Arizona, and credits for his military training, he would be able to graduate with his BS in General Science in June of 1964. This assured that he already had one degree in hand when he started Medical School in August of 1964. And Lisa had her Law Degree, so they were both ready to move on to Jackson where they would spend at least the next 4 years. For the first time there would be a few more loans available to him through independent banks and Lisa had applied and interviewed for jobs with several attorneys in the Jackson area. She was accepted by all three firms where she applied and finally decided to work for Smith, Smith and Farley.

Chapter 4
Medical School in Jackson, MS

JOE AND LISA MOVED to Jackson into a small middle class neighborhood just the other side of State Street behind the old movie theatre within 5 minutes walking of the medical school. The law firm of Smith, Smith and Farley was on North State Street just south of the old capitol building. She could either drop him at the university on the way to work or he could walk to class.

Joe knew full well what the first 2 years of medical school would require. It would be 8 hours of class daily except for the lunch break, actually 7 hours of lecture daily usually. Then you went to the library or home and you studied your lecture notes and the text book to learn the material you had covered that day. Depending on how fast you could read and retain material, you might be finished studying between 10 and 12 midnight that evening. Some of the courses he took that 1st year were Gross Anatomy, Micro Anatomy, and Physiology, as taught by the teacher of teachers Author Guyton, MD, whose textbook they also used. Seating in the lecture room was assigned by alphabet starting on the right end of the 1st row if you were facing the students. So Joe Ruff must have been seated near the back on the right. No one ever checked the role, but no one was ever absent because you couldn't cut classes and pass. You needed your notes plus the one class member's notes who was the designated class note taker. You see there were no CDs, or practice tests that one could buy or online anything and there were no special courses either. There were a few condensed versions of books around but by Joe's experience, the questions didn't come out of those books. They expected you to use your notes and the big textbook.

Remember there were no computers, iPhones, or internet in those days. You had to write it all down in longhand as you heard it. This would be a rude awakening to students in medical school these days. Whoever could listen and take the best set of notes had an extreme advantage. And this is not to mention that most of the lecturers were horrible speakers and lecturers. Too bad no one ever taught them how to teach. Joe surmised that would have made medical school much easier.

Here is a sample of the type of answers the student had to choose from in answering most questions that were asked.

(1) A and C are correct

(2) B and D are correct

(3) all are false

(4) all are true

(5) A is true

And if a possible answer read that 'always' or 'never' you could usually rule that one out. These tests were certainly a check on how precise your reading was.

There were certainly casualties at the end of the 1st year. Eleven, to be exact. Med school was no place to dally. If you didn't come there with a work ethic, you'd better find another line of work. So Joe's class started the second year with 69 students. There were also a few who had to go back and do a little more work in the summer, but the 69 survived to fight again. Really the school would try to keep you in school if you had a "git ur done" attitude. They would finally graduate with a class of 70 because they received another student their 3rd year, who had to repeat year three.

Now, just to be sure you were paying attention, you might be asked a question that was out of a recent journal article that was only casually mentioned in lecture. And the catch phrase might, in some questions, be 'sometimes or always.' Now try that one on for size. To say the least, study as hard as you may, when the test came it was a game of 'gotcha.' Joe was a straight-at-'cha kind of guy and at no place in his academic career had he had to play such games of the majestic's wizardry of the English language. He would learn, but it was not easy. Maybe 10% of the students were already up to speed on this kind of word magic, but it took the other 90% a while to catch on to this game.

It wasn't that Joe couldn't play this game. It was just that when flying high speed jet aircraft that kind of wizardry would just get you killed. There is little doubt why the Beechcraft Bonanza is well known as the 'doctor killer'. A Bonanza is the first thing many a young doctor wants as soon as he can save the pennies. He thinks that all you need to do is go buy a Beechcraft Bonanza, and since he's a good reader of medical books, take a few flying lessons and suddenly he's bullet proof. So what does he do but treat that aircraft as a benign toy. But the news story tomorrow may well be a story about how he got his whole family killed doing something he thought he should be able to learn by read-ing a book. Put another way, a doctor gives a patient a prescription and tells the patient that this medicine works on 70% of the patients. Some doctors might think that if you do it right 70% of the time in flying that's good enough. Well it's not because 30% of the time you run the risk of killing yourself and all those in the aircraft. Am I hitting home? The cemetery is full of dead doctors who thought that because they could read a medical book, the same should apply to flying. Flying is a noble profession and like the sea it is unforgiving when it comes to carelessness or complacency and that includes lack of experience.

So medical school was a bit different for Joe and most other stu-dents who had been taught that everything was not really spelled out in degrees of right and wrong. In medicine you might call that the prag-matic approach: it works in medicine some of the time but NEVER in flying high performance aircraft. And in RELATIVE terms the Bonan-za is a high performance aircraft.

Joe would never forget his pathology course in the 2nd year. Joe thought the Chair of the department was a strange, but good man. He invited all the class out to his home which was a small 5 acre place that had a one acre pond on it. He was a 55 year old bachelor. The guests were invited to swim and eat as a class mixer. Joe certainly enjoyed the day but when he left there was a core group that stayed until much later. Pretty soon Joe began to hear about the special invitation parties at the Chairman's house, though Joe never received one. That was okay with Joe because he and Lisa were always extremely busy with other interests. Lisa loved to see the new movies when they came town and there was the occasional office party they attended.

One day towards the end of the course the pathology lab instructor came in and handed each student a set of slides and said this is your final test in the lab part of the course. You are to look at all the slides and you are to write a report on what the disease process is, and you are not to collaborate with each other, that would be cheating, and if caught you will get a zero grade. Joe took that to heart, but throughout the course of about 2 weeks he could see the problem but was unable to make a diagnosis. In the meantime, many of the other students were collaborating in whispered voices. Joe did not. The instructor had made it clear to begin with that they were not to talk to or consult with each other.

You would never guess what happened. Joe was the ONLY ONE in the 69 who did not get the correct answer. Have you ever heard the old saying, cooperate and graduate? Joe ended up with a 75 grade for that course, which was of course a passing grade by 5 points. Joe would later find out that the ones who frequented the Chairman's ranch all made grades between 85 and 90. But Joe told Lisa that he wouldn't have done it any other way. He never looked on anyone else's paper in 4 years of medical school. What he made on any test was what he and he alone knew. He vied for excellence on his own. Every test he ever took in medical school, before or after, was his own work and his alone. If he couldn't make it without cheating he would rather not be there. That is the way he was taught and lived to this point and he wasn't going to change now.

Joe had known before going to medical school that the academics of the first two years was the hardest part of the four years, so he had resigned from the Air Guard just before starting his first year. His longer range plan was to get back in the Air Guard after finishing his second year of medical school. The third year was mostly seeing patients and learning to use the information you had learned the first two years.

The Jackson Air Guard at the time was flying the C121, super constellation aircraft, which was literally a white collar job. The aircraft was super clean and a real beauty to fly and even though it wasn't a jet, it was a fun machine to fly. It was air conditioned, even on the ground, and pressurized down to 2500 feet. It handled superbly and cruised at 240 knots true airspeed. It was clean, sleek and was not a dirty flying suit job. And Joe enjoyed flying this machine from the start. So Joe stayed on active duty most of the summer of 1966 going through all the squares and upgrading to Aircraft Commander. Finally by the end of the summer he had also flown two missions to Japan delivering much needed manpower and supplies for the troops in Viet Nam.

He would then return to his third year of medical school in late August of 1966, ready to begin using all that academia he had learned. All Joe's classmates knew he was an Air Force pilot and admired his contribution to his country. By the time one gets to the third year everyone knows most everyone else in the class and shared a special kind of friendship and respect for one another that most doctors do.

One of the things students were allowed to do, if you had extra time, was hang around the Emergency Room and watch and assist the interns and residents seeing patients. This was a very rewarding experience because one could see the things they had learned in academics put into practice. And you never knew what might come rolling through the door next, a stab wound, gunshot wound, or a motor vehicle accident with four or five serious injuries. All of the residents and interns had Emergency Room rotations as part of their training, and they would always welcome a new set of hands. Not every rotation was pleasant though. The Chief Resident in OB-GYN had been a PFC in the army before getting out of the service and going back to college. And he knew that Joe was a Captain in the Air Guard and never would make eye contact. Joe finally realized that he appeared to hate officers. He made sure Joe was watched and raked over the coals at every turn. Joe just kept his distance and sure enough he got a low grade. He learned that there are a few situations you can't control, so you have to just let go. This particular chief resident did have an unfortunate ending only five years after getting out into practice; he died quickly of a massive heart attack at the age of 38. But on a happier note, Joe liked OB-GYN because the doctor is there to help a young woman perform one of the really great miracles of life. And that is to help her bring new life into the world.

There are always a few things in those early clinical years that one never forgets. One was a 23-year-old man who had nearly no kidney function left because of diabetes. He effectively committed suicide by eating 45 bananas in one sitting. That sent his potassium level so high that he died shortly after being admitted to the hospital because the extremely high potassium level stopped his heart.

The 3rd year students were assigned patients on the various wards or floors on which they had to do a work up, that is history and physical, and then recommend orders. Joe would never forget the first patient he was assigned. She was an elderly colored female. Joe did the history part of his work up and then started a physical exam on her when she suddenly said, "Git you hands off me, I ain't gonna let you discover me." When Joe told the other students what had occurred, he was bent over in laughter. These types of occurrences were common in medicine. You had to laugh occasionally to keep your sense of balance. Probably any young doctor or any young pilot can tell similar stories.

The 3rd year of medical school was physically taxing and 3rd year students were required to run as many of their own lab tests as possible, like urine analysis or hematocrit for example. Joe would find the value of knowing how to do routine lab work later when he would need to teach his own office staff. Medical school is four years long for a reason; each year represents another progression in the making of a doctor. The same occurs in the progression and making of a USAF pilot. Also, that 3rd year represents the bottom of the totem pole in clinical medicine and no one wants to be there any longer than its takes to get through it. Once the medical student gets to the 4th year they begin to get a little respect and people begin to listen a little more to them. And that's a big lift from the 3rd year.

Joe was really glad to get that 3rd year behind him for more than one reason. And that was that he could spend more time flying and get more active duty days. And Lisa was adjusting well to law practice and frequently talked about her cases but without using names. Joe could tell she was enjoying her law practice.

In the Spring of 1966, Lisa went to Montana and brought Lee Ann back to Mississippi to live with her and Joe. Lee Ann had done well in grammar school in Montana and it was time for her to enter middle school and they wanted to enroll her in a private school near Jackson and become a real family. Joe and Lisa decided they would take Lee Ann for a week's vacation before she started to school. So they rented a pop-up camper and pulled it to the Smokey Mountains to camp.

Photo by www.otherpower.com[1]

THE FIRST THING THEY saw on the way to their campsite was, and you guessed it, a line of cars stopped on the side of the road and they were feeding the bears. There was no accident this time but the rangers told everyone not to feed the bears. Joe and Lisa already knew about the bear feeding first hand and shared that story with Lee Ann. The Smokey's, though only about a 5,000 foot elevation, still made it cool enough to relax and have an enjoyable time. The little town of Gatlinburg was just one short little street with a couple of hotels and a few shops. There was also a lift which would take you high enough to have a better view of the town area. There was a small ranger station near the entrance to the park, and camp sites were still 2 dollars per day. Pigeon Forge was there, but it was a relatively deserted and small place, as was Cherokee, N.C. on the other side of the mountains. There were also a few cabins for rent, but not many.

At the end of their week, Joe, Lisa and Lee Ann had cleaned up their campsite, as requested by the Park Rangers, folded up their rented tent camper and were heading out of the park when they approached a line of cars stopped on the side of the road. But people seemed to be

1. http://www.otherpower.com

running around hysterically. So Joe pulled over to the side, got out of the car and walked towards all the commotion and as soon as he got to the crowd he saw a woman lying on her back with deep scratches to her face and body and blood was spurting from her right femoral artery about two thirds of the way down towards her knee and everyone was screaming. Immediately Joe remembered seeing a stab wound just like that at the University Emergency Room. Everyone was screaming "She's bleeding to death!" Joe grabbed the handkerchief from his back pocket as he went down on his knees. He put the handkerchief around the thigh above where the blood was spurting, but was not able to get enough pressure by twisting the handkerchief to stop the bleeding. He knew this was a now or never situation and he knew he had to stop the bleeding. He asked a man who was standing nearby to please bring him that stick that he saw on the side of the road. Joe inserted the stick into the handkerchief and twisted it gradually tighter until the bleeding stopped. It took the ambulance another 12 minutes to arrive and with Joe still holding pressure on the tourniquet, he and the patient were loaded into the ambulance. Lisa and Lee Ann followed the ambulance and once they arrived at the Emergency Room of the hospital Joe turned the patient over to the doctor who was waiting.

The woman's husband then related to Joe the story of what had happened. She had been feeding a bear and everything was going well until she ran out of food. At that instant, the bear became angry because he wanted more food. And what came next was a vicious attack of biting and clawing and he finally bit her thigh as he shook her in his mouth. It was fortunate for the injured woman that Joe had recently seen that same sort of stab wound to the thigh in the University Emergency Room.

The whole trip was one of laid back relaxation except for the last scene. Also Joe and Lisa would remember it in a positive way because Lisa became pregnant on this trip. Soon after their return to Jackson they would learn of their new arrival to be due in January of 1968, Joe's senior year of medical school.

When Joe returned to Jackson he would be going through Aircraft Commander check out in none other than the C124, called "Old Shaky" for a good reason. Everything about it vibrated. And it was another dirty flying suit job, anything but the "white collar" job that the C121 had been. It was loud, and everything you touched vibrated and got your hands dirty. It was hot inside and out in the summer and cold inside and out in the winter. Also, it was slow, cruising at about 180-190 knots. Joe had never heard a pilot say he loved "Old Shaky". Now for the positive side of the job, it would haul almost anything. It had big clamshell doors on the front and you could drive a vehicle inside and haul it; or you could haul a whole company of troops and gear. No doubt about it, it was a master hauler and that's why the Air Force forced them onto the pilots. It would do more of what they wanted than the C121. Meanwhile they continued to make trips to Japan and Asia in support of the war effort during Joe's senior year of medical school. Joe had a little more time to participate in the Air Guard during his senior year of medical school than he had before. One thing was for sure; the Air Guard was worth its weight to the Air Force. It did more than its part of the heavy lifting. They sent those planes anywhere and everywhere and anytime the Air Force needed help with the heavy lifting, the Air Guard was always ready to do its part.

One of the highlights of Joe's senior year was when he had the pleasure of flying a C124 to San Diego to interview for a surgical residency program. When word got out about that in the senior medical class, there were 11 other seniors who were already commissioned officers due to go in the military at the end of the 4th year. Joe had the permission of the commanding officer on the unit to allow them to ride along. He planned to make stops in Phoenix and San Diego to look at internships and residencies.

All of them showed up for the long ride in " Old Shaky" and Joe personally checked their ID's to be sure they were legal. They departed the Jackson, Mississippi airport at 8 am on a Thursday and arrived in Phoenix, Arizona at Sky Harbour Airport in the afternoon. They unloaded and went to a Holiday Inn where one of the hospitals would pick them up Saturday morning and transport them to the first hospital for them to see and be interviewed. They all looked at St. Joseph's and Good Samaritan hospitals and then they went on and looked at Maricopa General hospital. In the late afternoon they all took off once again in "Old Shaky" and headed west to San Diego.

They arrived about 9:00 pm, well after dark, landing to the west over the power lines. Because of the steep terrain just to the east of the field, it was a particularly steep approach. No sweat though, Joe just stuck to the planned approach and held the airspeed on the money and made a good landing. After parking and unloading, everyone was told what time they would be departing and what time to show up. Joe had a special invitation from the Chief of Surgery, Captain Walker, for lunch at his home on Sunday. Joe and his other pilot friend looked at the Balboa Naval Hospital and talked with the chief surgery resident and the situation appeared promising. At lunch that day Captain Walker told Joe that he was inviting him to join their general surgery internship and residency program. Joe responded with, "Thank you Sir, I will need to discuss this with my wife."

Joe and all his guests and crew met back at the aircraft on Sunday afternoon at 3:00 pm. All were present and accounted for. After pre-flighting the aircraft, they all boarded, the loadmaster closed all the doors and hatches and Joe went to the end of the runway. Takeoff would be to the east. Joe got Air Traffic Control Instrument Flight Rules Clearance and the tower cleared him onto the runway but told him to hold until the flight that had just landed cleared the active runway. Then the San Diego tower said, "cleared for takeoff" and Joe pushed the power on all four engines to max power and they were off and rolling down the runway. He approached lift off speed, lifted off and retracted the gear soon afterward. Then at a predetermined speed Joe told the copilot to retract the flaps.

They were about 2 miles out on takeoff with an altitude of 1,000 feet at climb power and climbing when suddenly the #3 engine began to backfire and lost oil pressure. Before Joe could tell the engineer to feather (shut down) the engine the loadmaster reported seeing flames coming out of the same engine. Joe had already switched to approach control. Joe declared an emergency while he was making a left turn to a downwind leg for runway 09 at 1500 feet altitude and returned to San Diego tower frequency and notified them of his emergency and his intent to make a left base leg over the water and make a three engine landing on runway 09 to the east. The fire on #3 engine had stopped as soon as the engine was shut down. The aircraft was maneuvered into final approach so Joe just made a 3 engine landing to the east on runway 09 like he had done so many times in the flight simulator. They were fortunate that they did not have a heavy load at the time: or they would have had an even larger problem.

Once on the ground, shut down and unloaded, Joe, the copilot and the engineer made a closer assessment of the engine area and decided that there was no structural damage to the aircraft from the fire. Joe then went to the nearest phone and called General McFarland, made his report and the general said, "I'm proud of you Joe. I'll have another C124 out there with a new engine tomorrow afternoon and you and your group can return home in that aircraft. So one day later than scheduled Joe and his group landed back in Jackson, Mississippi, a day late but safe and sound.

The Medical School was abuzz with all the news about the great trip they had been a part of and how they had landed back in San Diego with an engine failure. For Joe though, this was just another day at the office. As one pilot might say to another, "That's why we draw flight pay. Its part of the job."

This was late November of 1967, Lisa was now 7 months into her pregnancy and she had actually gained very little weight other than the baby which, at this point, was about 5 pounds. In the meantime Joe and Lisa had bought their first home in the North Jackson area. Also this year was only the second Super Bowl and Joe and Lisa would watch it on the same old black and white TV, the same one they had from years ago. Some people already had color televisions and the student lounge at the school also had one. It was a Zenith made in the U.S. The old TVs had vertical stability problems where if it became slightly out of sync the picture would start tumbling. But at the time it was a brand new technology and made in the U.S.A. As the years went on they would become better and more reliable. Then the Japanese got into the act and were able to build better TVs at a cheaper price and pretty soon the American made TVs disappeared from the market never to return.

Joe and Lisa kicked around the idea of a straight surgery internship at San Diego or Phoenix and there was also the possibility of an internship at the University of Mississippi, right there in Jackson, or the possibility of doing the internship at Baptist Hospital, also in Jackson. The one at the University might provide more experience at all levels but the one at Baptist would provide more and better experience in how the doctors out in the community actually practiced their art; plus the internship at Baptist Hospital would pay much better.

So, after all due consideration, including that Lee Ann would not have to change schools again and get used to a whole new environment and group of friends, Joe and Lisa elected to stay in Jackson and do his internship at Mississippi Baptist hospital where Joe did rotations on Cardiology, Internal Medicine, Orthopedics, Surgery and Emergency Medicine. He especially enjoyed his rotation on Cardiology. Dr. Rosenfeld did exercise tests for the heart. Those tests would consist of so many trips over the steps and back, dependent on age of the patient. The cardiologist would look for depression or elevation of the S-T segment of the EKG to see if there was a cardiac problem. Also if the patient had any chest pain or significant shortness of breath the test would be stopped.

On January 31st, 1968, Joe and Lisa's first born, Cindy, was born. She was a beautiful baby and the whole family was excited. Joe was especially excited about this child, as he hadn't had much contact with his first two children. He supported them from the time they were born, but hadn't seen much of them at all.

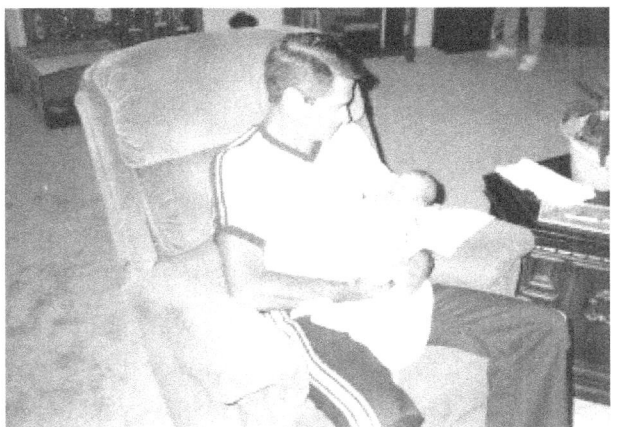

Author photo

JUST WHEN JOE WAS FEELING pretty relaxed in the Emergency Room rotation Hurricane Camille came blasting through Gulfport, Mississippi about the middle of May 1969.

Pixabay.com free images

JOE WAS ON DUTY THAT day in the Emergency Room. The hospitals in south Mississippi were filled rapidly and Baptist Hospital Emergency room was full of patients. It was mostly people hit by flying debris and that usually makes an ugly wound. The staff knew when the storm hit that they must be prepared for the worst. They saw a number of fractured arms and legs and severe lacerations of the scalp and face. It was fortunate that they saw it coming and had enough notice to have all hands on deck when the patients started arriving about 4:00 in the afternoon. Joe sutured a severed laceration of the scalp and found from the lab that the patient had bled so much on the scene that she only had a hemoglobin of 8 and thus needed 2 units of blood and more IV fluids.

There was also one patient who had been hit in the chest with flying debris. The patient had extreme shortness of breath and chest pain. After getting a stat chest X-ray Joe diagnosed a pneumothorax, put in a chest tube and set up suction to reinflate the lung on that side, then sent the patient to intensive care for monitoring.

During 1969 and 1970 Joe and Lisa had two more babies, first another girl, Lindy, and then a boy, Donald. They were now a family of six.

Chapter 5
York, Alabama Practice

JOE DID NOT LIKE OWING money on student loans and he was anxious about that, so he decided after his internship at Baptist that he would look for a place to do general practice in Mississippi or Alabama, where he would also be licensed. He and Lisa would ultimately decide to move to the small town of York, AL because it was close to where Joe grew up, although he also considered Jackson, Butler, and Livingston, Alabama as well, and it was a small town environment which would be better for the children.

When Joe and Lisa ultimately moved to York, he was one of three physicians and the other physicians were as busy as they wanted to be. The hospital was located about 100 yards from all three doctors' offices. The hospital was only a thirty bed hospital but it offered most of the services routinely needed by the patient. It served good food and the hospital administrator was a retired Navy Commander who knew how a hospital should be run. So, Dr. Ruff had a patient clientele already waiting. He appreciated the fine support he received from the town administration and town folk.

There were actually two hospitals in the county, one in York and one in the town of Livingston, which was 8 miles north of York. Livingston, was a somewhat larger town and also the county seat, where the courthouse was located. Livingston had about 3500 inhabitants and York had about 2500. There was an unusual competitiveness between these two little towns that Joe never quite understood. If one town built something like a new hospital, the other one had to see if they could out do the first. Different towns and different family names made for an abundance of hostility between the two towns. Since Livingston had the county seat and a small University of about 800 or 900 students, it seemed to be maybe economically ahead, but there were plenty of good, well- meaning people in both communities who were willing to do anything to help the people of their own town. But what was good for one community in the end was really good for both on a county-wide basis. So Joe and Lisa moved into York, Alabama with their two children and set up shop there.

Joe would never forget the first patient he saw in the York Hospital Emergency room. It was a 14 year old colored boy who had been hit across his right scapula area with an ax by his brother in a fit of rage. In doing so he had cut his brother's scapula (shoulder blade) completely in half. To be honest, Joe had never seen this same injury before but common sense dictated that if it was cut completely into two parts, you had to figure a way to put it back where it was in a manner that would enable it to stay. Dr. Joe knew that he had to have some large suture material and a large needle that would go through soft bone. So, he asked the nurse for No.2 Prolene suture on the largest needle they had. While she was getting the suture and the suture pack out, Dr. Joe deadened the whole area with 1% lidocaine and cleaned it with Betadine. He also gave the boy a tetanus toxoid injection. Joe then made several interrupted sutures through the scapula bone, being careful to put the bone back exactly as it had been before the injury.

Dr. Joe saw the young man back in the office the following day and again in a week to get the skin sutures out. All ended well and Dr. Joe treated it like any other fracture and in six weeks he was as good as new. And Dr. Joe assumed the boy's mother told both brothers to refrain from playing with axes, especially if they were angry at one another.

Dr. Joe decided in the early going that he would open a satellite office in the township of Lauderdale which was 12 miles from York to the west. It would be an afterhours clinic at which he would see a few patients after office hours 3 days each week. There was only one problem and that was there was no place to have a clinic except in an old feed room across the road from the General Store. The feed room was where they had kept feed for the farm animals but they were no longer using it. There was no exam table, only a straight-back chair for Joe to sit in and another straight-back chair facing the doctor for the patient. Dr Joe operated this little clinic on a cash basis and used his house-call bag as both his diagnostic and pharmacy kit. He was able to give injections when needed and of course he had his stethoscope, otoscope and ophthalmoscope, a percussion hammer, etc. He might see three patients or as many as 6 or 7 on the busiest days. He had no nurse with him so he took the vital signs on all patients himself.

As long as he lived, Dr. Joe would never forget one particular patient he saw. She was a small plump colored lady who came in late one afternoon. She said she had no money but would be sure she brought money the next trip she made. Dr. Joe said fine, its not about the money anyway. If you want to be seen I would see you without the money. So she gave a history of blood pressure problems and Dr. Joe proceeded to examine her. He checked her blood pressure and then stuck his stethoscope inside her dress to listen to her heart. And just as he did, a huge roll of bills fell out of her bosom and onto her lap. She and Dr. Joe looked at each other and both just hollered, they were laughing so loud. It was funny, the things that sometimes happen in a country practice setting. Dr. Joe still did not demand payment that day. She was one of those types that liked paying for last week's visit today. In other words, she always paid, but one visit later.

Finally Dr. Joe got that little after-hours practice going so well that the country store owner decided to put a twenty foot trailer, with A/C and heating next to his store. Then Dr. Joe put in a pharmacy complete with pill counter, waiting room and one exam room. Dr. Joe ran that little after- hours practice for years after that and finally got to the point where he had to take his nurse with him. Dr. Joe learned from this experience that perception is everything. If people see you as being hard working and a straight shooter they will come. And if they see you as caring for them they will be hanging from the rafters to see you.

Meanwhile, Dr. Joe's practice in York continued to grow. One thing Dr. Joe thought they really needed was an Intensive Care Unit in the York Hospital. The Administrator was approached about this but he really didn't understand the need. So, Dr. Joe and the other 2 doctors discussed it with him at the staff meetings but according to administrator the idea was just too costly. So the administrator did what he thought was a compromise. He put a cardiac monitor in one of the patient rooms which gave an electrocardiogram tracing on the screen. Only problem was, the patient could follow his heart tracing, but there was no monitor at the nursing station. The obvious question was, how does it help to have a cardiac monitor at the patients bedside if there is no monitor at the nursing station? Is the patient suppose to notify the nurse if there is a problem? Well, that ended in hard feelings between the administrator and Dr. Joe even though it could not be helped. It started a spitting contest about something that didn't need to happen. One thing led to another and finally Dr. Joe decided to look into the hospital located 8 miles up the road at Livingston. They were a friendly bunch and of the two, at the moment, they seemed to be doing the best job of the hospital end of it. Dr. Joe was delivering a lot of babies and doing a lot of what you might call "bread and butter surgery" including hemorrhoid, hernia, appendectomy and gallbladder surgeries. Livingston had the best physical plant and nursing staff at the time and within a year of starting there, Dr. Joe had all the business he could manage.

Even though there were bent feelings, Joe kept his group of golf playing buddies in York. He had a regular group with whom he played.

And they would be friends for a long time to come. There was Red Graves, Coon Robb, Justin Orland, who walked with a limp, Carl Hargrove, Justin Barnes and Billy Lee Williams who was the finest 19-year-old golfer that Dr. Joe had ever seen. Dr. Joe even offered to sponsor him on the pro tour, but young Williams turned the offer down.

Carl Hargrove was a 30-year-old, strong, athletic guy who had been raised in York and was an excellent golfer. His Dad had owned the General Store in downtown York for many years before retiring and selling the store to one of his lifelong employees Fred Kelso. The elder Hargrove had also left a sizable amount of money to his son Carl, along with 10,000 acres of the finest pine timber one could ever imagine. Fred was a good person and Dr. Joe knew him well. Too bad his wife ran off with another man from just across the Mississippi line.

One Monday afternoon Carl Hargrove came running into Dr. Joe's office with a suit case. Dr. Joe summoned him to go to his private office and when Carl opened that suitcase it was full of $100 dollar bills to the tune of $143,000. Dr. Joe said, "Where did all that money come from?" Carl said, "I won it playing baccarat in Las Vegas." Dr. Joe's immediate response was, "DON'T GO BACK! This is a set up. Those people aren't rich on gambling for nothing." Unfortunately Carl did not take Dr. Joe's advice. Two months later he was clear cutting all that virgin pine timber off his 10,000 acres and as far as Dr. Joe knew he didn't stop until he was completely broke. Dr. Joe would later in life learn that Carl had finally become a golf pro at a small country club in south Alabama.

It just so happened that Dr. Joe's Dad had a 1400 acre farm just 30 miles north of York, AL which was loaded with quail. Over the course of a couple of years Joe had met and become friends with one of only two lawyers in the county of Sumpter. His name was Don Priester the 3rd and he was in practice with his father. It was a tight knit circle and both Dr. Joe and Don liked that Jack Daniels Black Label. They had some great times together cooking out with their wives and kids while having a few drinks. The Priesters also had children about the same age as Dr. Joe and Lisa's.

One day Dr. Joe's Dad told him that a man who lived in Shuqualak, MS, which was only about 40 miles from York, had a litter of Pointer bird dog puppies and he wanted Dad to have one of them. In case you don't know where that little town is, it is just 50 miles north of Meridian, MS and Dr. Joe's Dad's farm, or ranch if you prefer, was within 10 miles of there. He told Joe's Dad to just stop by and pick one out of the pen and take it home. Dr. Joe and his Dad did stop and Joe picked out a pretty little white female with orange ears. She was a nice looking pup and the man had told Joe's Dad that she was out of "Gunsmoke" breeding, which if you know anything about bird dog breeding is a very famous blood line. Anyway, Joe's Dad didn't want the puppy so he gave her to Joe. One month later when Dr. Joe and his Dad were hunting quail on his Dad's place, they were walking along, following the older dogs, when they noticed "Birdie", as Joe had named her, standing on a ditch bank, frozen as solid as a statue. Joe's Dad suddenly said, "I think that puppy may be pointing a bird". Joe agreed.

Author photo

AND AS THEY GOT WITHIN a few feet, a quail flew and Dad killed it. Birdie ran about 40 feet out, picked up the bird and brought it to them. She was just 12 weeks of age and that was when Joe knew he had a real bird dog. You can't teach these dogs to do that, it's instinct., and they either have it or they don't. She never proved over the years to be a wide ranging hunter like some of the field trial dogs. She simply hunted about 50 yards out and found all the birds that those wild running dogs missed. And any time Joe shot down a bird she would always find it and retrieve.

Dr. Joe's Dad had an old black and white English setter that was an excellent bird dog as well. His name was "Cotton". He was a medium ranger and the combination of Cotton and Birdie was unbeatable. When those two dogs were with you, if you didn't kill plenty of birds it was your own fault. And since the farm was quite large, you could always go out and find 4 or 5 covies of quail within an hour or two.

Joe and his law friend, Don Priester, hunted a lot together and he was a good shot. He killed a bird about every other shot. Dr. Joe must have felt sorry for the birds because his accuracy was more like one in 3 or 4 shots. Oh well, Joe always had a negative feeling about killing anything. He really would rather leave that to the owls and hawks. The thing he loved about quail hunting was watching the quail dogs work. They, like all professionals, come in all different varieties of talent.

Dr. Joe bought two white and black setter puppies out of "Mr. Thor", a well known championship trials dog. Dr. Joe had built a bird-dog pen in his backyard complete with houses and a 30 foot run. Joe remembered he had bought another black and white pointer from a man in Jackson that was also out of high blood lines. But the first time he took her into the field and she heard gunfire she broke point and ran under the truck. She was "gun shy" and don't you know that man knew that before he sold her to Dr. Joe. Well those things happen sometimes in dog trading, as well as horse trading. It was just a hazard of being in the business.

Dr. Joe also got into buying recently hatched birds for the purpose of training his dogs. The way this works is that you go out in the field and plant the birds and let the puppy find them. That way you know where the bird is and it's the job of the puppy to find it; and in this way you can train and separate the best puppies from the ones who are not going to make the cut. This was really the part of quail hunting that Dr. Joe loved. Truth be known, he didn't like killing anything.

Don Priester was also an avid deep sea fisherman and had his own fishing boat anchored in Destin, Florida, with its own captain to conduct the fishing trips. He went on a regular basis to Destin and fished for marlin and sailfish. He and his wife invited Dr. Joe and Lisa to go with them and they accepted the invitation. Joe's mother had volunteered to take the children while they were gone. The four left York and

Livingston at noon on a Friday arriving at Destin about 5:00 pm. The fishing gear was already on the boat and the captain took care of the food and drink for the Saturday fishing trip, except for the Jack Daniels which Don provided.

They got to the hotel rooms that they had reserved and hung their belongings. Then off to dinner they went to one of the seaside restaurants along the wharf where all the fishing boats were parked, getting ready for tomorrow's fishing trips. The boats and the restaurants were within just a few feet of each other and the hotel was only 50 yards away. After eating a great seafood dinner the four listened to the band that was playing on the wharf and danced a few licks. After that, they retired in order to get some rest before tomorrow's big fishing trip. Joe and Lisa had called Joe's mother to check on the kiddies and to let them know where they could be reached if needed.

The next morning, Saturday, they all went to the boat and Captain Johns was already there. He had food of all sorts and plenty of soft drinks and the foursome had brought their own beer and Jack Daniels. By 6:30 am everyone was loaded up and the captain headed out to deep water. This was sport fishing for the big fish and to do it one had to go to the deeper water at least 5-10 miles out. Once they were out there, Don and Joe put out the bait that Captain Johns had specified they use and started trolling slowly. Over the first 30 minutes there were no strikes so Captain Johns went to a different fishing hole a few miles away and also changed the bait. It wasn't 3 minutes before Joe had a strike and immediately the fish came out of the water and it was a nice size sailfish. Then the battle was on. That fish ran to the side and came out of the water again and each time there was a little slack Joe would reel it in. This continued over about 17 minutes and finally with Joe reeling in a little slack at a time he finally had the fish along the side of the boat. Capt. Johns then grabbed the line with a hook and brought the fish into the boat. The fish weighed in at 72 pounds.

Once again the fishermen put their troll lines out and it was another 10 minutes before Don had a strike. It literally bent his rod double. One could see that he had a huge fish hooked and finally about 20 seconds later the fish made his first jump and it was a huge marlin, Don's favorite sports fish. It appeared to weigh at least 250-300 pounds. And the fight was just beginning. That fish jumped again and again not giving an inch. It was apparent that they would have to see who gave out first. Don looked as though he was in a fight for his life and every time that fish came out of the water he was headed the other way. What a fight. Don had told Joe in advance that if you hooked a fish like that it was a battle of the wills and minds of the fisherman and the fish. Never had Joe seen such a battle in his life. After about 15 minutes Don had the fish within 100 feet of the boat when the line broke. "Wow", Don said, "all that work for a broken line." Captain Johns said that this was common if the fish was large enough and the fish sensed the slightest slack in the line. Nothing lost, just the hook and bait. So the captain put on a fresh hook and new bait on Don's line and continued trolling.

The next strike was about 10 minutes later when Don had another strike. This time it was another large fish and when he came out of the water about 175 yards out it was another huge marlin, maybe 200 pounds, not quite as large as the last one. They managed to get him inside 100 yards before Joe had a strike on his line and again it was a large marlin. So, now they had two battles going on at the same time. Now Don had gotten his fish within 100 feet of the boat and was hanging on for dear life. Anyone could tell he was worn out. Meanwhile, Joe's fish was out there at about 150 yards and when he came out of the water Captain Johns estimated his weight at 175 pounds. Don now had his fish within 50 feet of the boat and estimated his weight to be about 250 pounds. It took another 10 minutes to get Don's fish in the boat and Joe now had his fish within 100 feet of the boat. As one might think, there was lots of noise and cheerleading from the girls on the boat when Captain Johns finally weighed Don's fish at 254 pounds. Joe now had his marlin inside 50 feet of the boat. After about another 5 minutes of fighting, Captain Johns finally pulled Joe's fish aboard and weighed him in at 217 pounds. Everyone aboard was ecstatic over the events of the day and the fish they had caught. But Don and Joe were worn completely out and ready for a good cool drink and a cold shower. Since all were tired and hot, Captain Johns took up a compass heading of north because they were far out of site of land. After a few minutes on a magnetic compass heading of north they could once again see the shore line of Destin. After parking the boat in its usual spot and seeing the large catch, many people came to see exactly what they had caught and were asking about where they were caught. Everyone answered with the biggest lie they could think of as to where they had been. Ain't no lie like a good fishing lie, right?

One afternoon about 5:30 pm a nurse at the Livingston hospital called Dr. Joe to advise him that there was an OB patient there who was full term and needed a doctor to deliver her baby. She said that the patient was about 5 centimeters dilated with contractions about every 5 minutes. She thought the baby was coming soon. Dr. Joe drove immediately to the

hospital and by the time he checked the mother she was about 8 centimeters dilated and 80% effaced. Fetal heart tones were 180 beats per minute. She was a gravita 2. He and the nurse rolled her right into the delivery room, moved her over to the delivery table and put her up in the stirrups and by the time she was prepped and the Dr. had scrubbed, the baby was about ready to crown. Within 3 minutes Dr. Joe and the nurse had delivered what appeared to be a healthy 8 or 9 pound baby without any complications. The baby was sent to the nursery and the mother was sent to the floor. The placenta appeared normal and there was minimal blood loss during delivery.

The next day the same nurse took the healthy baby to the mother to allow the mother and baby to have time together. When the nurse returned about 10 minutes later to get the baby it was dead. The nurse asked the mother when it stopped breathing or if anything unusual had happened and the mother refused to answer. Dr. Joe was called and came to the hospital and asked the mother the same question and again she would not answer. Then Dr. Joe asked her if she had suffocated the baby and she just looked down. Dr. Joe had no choice but to call the authorities. The police became involved and the result was that the mother was charged with suffocating her baby. Dr. Joe was also called to testify in Circuit Court and he told the same story to the court. He later heard that there was a guilty verdict but the final outcome he never knew.

Joe had recently rejoined the Air National Guard because he missed flying. He had gotten out of the Guard several years before because he just could not find the time to participate. He was determined to get back to flying though. He had even recently bought an old C-model Bonanza. It had almost no radios in it though. He found some used radios for sale in Oklahoma City and decided to fly over there to get them installed. He did this on a Friday afternoon. It took a day or two for the installation. When he started the engine to go back to York it would not develop enough power to fly. He pulled back into the hangar area and shut it down. The man who was the owner and chief technician checked it over and told Joe it was a no go and would need a new rebuilt engine. Joe said, "Let's get 'er done." The man's name was Rex. This whole process took a whole week with Joe standing on one foot and then the other.

Finally after a week of waiting, the new engine was installed and Joe took off for York, getting home to Lisa and the kids after a 3 day excursion which turned into 10 days. The engine ran well on the way home but appeared to be a little sluggish at times. Joe thought it would loosen up a bit after a few hours of running. He was also to learn that the Bendix radios that he had bought were anything but reliable. Joe could not really complain though. He knew they were cheapies when he bought them.

About two weeks later Joe would fly the family down to Destin for a weekend of relaxation. After the weekend of relaxing on the beach with Lisa and the kids, they were off and bound for home. Forty miles out of York the new engine began to lose power. Joe started pushing the throttle up but it continued to lose power. He then pushed the RPM lever forward and there was still no response and the engine was constantly getting slower and now his airspeed was beginning to drop. When it finally dropped to 2000 RPM at full power he was really concerned. And to make matters even worse he was now over nothing but virgin pine forest with no place to put this baby down. He told Lisa what was going on and that he hoped we ran out of forest before they ran completely out of power and airspeed. They were fortunate that this time they out lasted the forest and limped in barely over the tree tops to the York airport. Or, as one might say, 'on a wing and a prayer.'

When Joe got out of that airplane he was as mad as a wet hen. As soon as he got home he called Rex in Oklahoma City and you don't want to hear what he told him. Anyway, Rex was down there in York the next morning on the first flight out of Oklahoma City. He went over the engine and when he had finished his inspection he said that the tech who had done the work on the engine heads put undersized valve guides in the heads because he didn't have the correct size. That caused the valve stems to overheat and expand. So what Joe really had was an engine that was trying to seize, or stop completely, and that was not a good thing. Dr. Joe told Rex not to touch the aircraft any further, that he had almost cost the life of Joe and his whole family.

Joe took the aircraft to a reputable facility in Montgomery, AL where the heads were redone and there was never another problem with that engine. But there was another problem with the C-model Bonanza; and that was that it would not comfortably carry Joe's whole family. It had a Continental engine that only had 205 HP, not to mention that two adult people with their luggage was a full load for the aircraft. In spite of what some might say, the C-model Bonanza simply was not designed to carry more than two people and their luggage. After discussing all this with Lisa, the two of them agreed they should sell this Bonanza and buy a larger one later. The next month Dr. Joe was able to find a buyer and sold it.

Chapter 6
Emergency Medicine Practice & Flight Surgeon

ALONG ABOUT THIS TIME Joe had been tied down in his country practice for 8 to 9 years and had been on 24/7 call for the whole time. He was beginning to wonder if the stress of all this was worth the money he was making. Once patients found out where he lived and in which bedroom he slept, they began to knock on his bedroom window at 2 and 3 am on a regular basis. He loved many of the good people of York and Livingston but the pressure was just bringing him to the breaking point. He simply couldn't say 'No' when someone needed him. Other doctors seemed to be able to limit their availability, but he couldn't. If he was in town or at home they would find him.

Finally after much soul searching and conversation with Lisa, he decided to shut down his practice in York and Livingston and go into Emergency Medicine which at this time was just now emerging as a speciality on its own. He already had plenty of offers for work. Also one of his old flying buddies from the Air Guard called. His friend, Lt. Col. Biffle O. Pittman, had just been made commander of the 153rd Air Reconnaissance Squadron in Meridian, Mississippi, which was only 30 miles away. He wanted Joe to come back in the unit as one of their flight surgeons. They currently had one other flight surgeon processing into the squadron. Biff told Joe that he would need to attend the Brookes Flight Surgeon School in San Antonio, Texas for 10 weeks.

Joe decided that this would be a great opportunity to finish out his 20 in the Air Force and provide a guaranteed retirement, so he told his friend he was on and he soon left for the school. In the meantime Joe had moved Lisa and the four children to Meridian, so he would base his Emergency Practice out of Meridian and the Air Guard was there in Meridian as well.

Joe worked Emergency Medicine over most of the state. Emergency Medicine was a budding speciality at the time. When patients came into the Emergency Room they were always asked whether or not they had a family doctor. Most of them did have a regular family doctor so after collecting all the information from the patient, the nurse would call the patient's family doctor to find out if he or she wanted to come see the patient or if they wanted the ER doctor to see and treat the patient. That was the standard protocol in all the ERs at that time. Or there might be one doctor taking call for a group of doctors. In any event the attending doctor had to be called on all patients unless the doctor had instructed the ER personnel otherwise. The rules varied a little from hospital to hospital.

Joe remembered very well that Baptist Hospital in Jackson, where Dr. Joe had trained, had a rule that any patient who didn't have a regular doctor would be treated by the Emergency Room doctor. You have to first understand that Jackson, MS is a fairly large town of about 200,000 population and that it was a University town as well, so everything was very specialized.

One Saturday about noon Joe was working the ER when the ambulance brought in a stabbing victim. He was a colored guy about 30 years old and his girlfriend had in anger taken a butcher knife and done a fine job of carving him up. Well this was nothing out of the ordinary for Dr. Joe. He had been there and done this numerous times out in the country. He assessed all the wounds and found that although there was a lot of sewing work to do, none of the wounds had penetrated the lungs or abdomen. The patient had, however, at least 10 lacerations 5-6 inches long scattered over his abdomen, face, and back. He was certainly an ugly looking mess.

Once Dr. Joe had ascertained there were no serious deep lacerations, he started closing the wounds. With many long lacerations he elected to do a running suture with 4-0 silk. After about 30 minutes he was about half finished with the job when he noticed the administrator and a couple of doctors looking on from the outside. He was a bit puzzled by this. Anyway he went on and finished the job and he had done a really nice job on this patient and in good time. But did his girlfriend do a good slashing job on him or what? When Dr. Joe finished he was sitting at the desk completing the paper work when one of the nurses revealed that the administrator and doctors were concerned as to why Dr. Joe had not asked for a plastic surgeon to see the patient. Dr. Joe responded, "I didn't need one. Where I've been working this is just all in a days work." The patient had a normal and full recovery.

Dr. Joe had another notable experience in another hospital in the Brandon, MS hospital ER. It came at 3:30 one morning. The Police Academy brought one of their students in to the emergency room with the complaint that his blood sugar was high. Dr. Joe ordered a complete blood count, a urinalysis and a blood sugar. All lab work was normal except for a high blood sugar of 230, which was high, but not outrageous. The patient said he wanted admission to the hospital. Dr. Joe asked where was his home and he responded, "Natchez", which was about 100 miles away. Dr. Joe said he could not justify admitting him to the hospital but that he would give him 10 units of regular insulin, which he did. He also told him to see his family doctor the next morning.

What Dr. Joe would learn later was that this man didn't like the school he was attending and wanted to go home to Natchez. Anyway, what this man did was go back to Natchez, eat a whole lot of sugar, enough to shoot his blood sugar very high, and then he went to the Natchez Hospital ER. So, when they checked his blood sugar it was over 600. He then filed a lawsuit against Dr. Joe and Dr. Joe's attorney insisted on settling with him for $8500. Dr. Joe had done nothing wrong but the lawyers got to divide up the $8500 so that they all got a payday. *That was really Dr. Joe's first experience in Law 101. Dr. Joe had committed no wrong, no malpractice, yet his lawyer insisted on a small settlement none the less because everybody gets a little something for their time, including the two lawyers and the plaintiff. Never mind that Dr. Joe gets a black mark on his record when he has not committed any malpractice.* And everyone is supposed to be happy. Lisa was absolutely livid. She said, Before I'll let you go through this again, I will defend you myself!"

Dr. Joe would be remiss not to tell you the ending of his dealings with the man mentioned in the above paragraph. Ten years later Dr. Joe was back in school, yes, this time in Psychiatry, at the University in Jackson, MS. He was on call that day for hospital psychiatry consults from the medical floors. He answered a consult on a medical patient and when Dr. Joe walked into the room, guess who was the patient. It was the same patient who sued Dr. Joe about his blood sugar. The patient did not recognize Dr. Joe but Joe had not forgotten that face. It was him alright and Dr. Joe even asked him if he had ever had diabetes and the patient said no. Joe could hardly keep from bursting out in laughter. And Joe learned from that, that it is a small world indeed.

Dr. Joe's ER work would take him all over Mississippi and Alabama. One of the places he worked was Fort Payne, Alabama. It was a medium sized hospital of about 75 beds. He worked there several times and the hospital administration and the staff doctors were well pleased with his work. One thing led to another and finally the hospital wanted him full time. It was a moderately busy ER for those days. The ER saw about 55 patients a day or about 20,000 patients per year, which was moderately busy. It only took about 6 months before Dr. Joe was asked to be the ER director and was also was given a company car to drive. It was a long haul from Meridian, MS to Ft. Payne, AL, about 210 miles.

It was a drive of 3 1/2 hrs. one way but Joe worked long shifts, 72 hours to be exact, so he only had to drive it once a week. He worked from Monday, 7:00 am thru Thursday at 7:00 am. Then he was off until the following Monday. He was happy with his schedule because it was a regular schedule and he knew that when he was off he was completely off and not subject to being called out. This also worked well with his air guard schedule now that he was one of two flight surgeons in this particular unit.

Dr. Joe thought by now he had seen about everything there was to see in general medicine and the Emergency Room. But that wasn't so. He was working the ER one hot July day when the ambulance brought in a 22-year-old construction worker whom they said had "fallen out" on the job. His vital signs revealed a temperature of 105 F degrees. Immediately Dr. Joe knew this was a nonstarter. He quickly pulled out his big ER medicine book and of course it said you'd better get him cooled down in a hurry. They happened to have a full body whirlpool next to the ER in physical therapy. He ordered the whirlpool to be quickly filled with water while adding ice. He then had the patient inserted into the whirlpool and added as much ice as possible. It was about 20 minutes before his temperature began to fall. It took about an hour before the patient's temperature finally reached 100 degrees and at that point Dr. Joe had him out of the whirlpool and into one of the examining rooms where he monitored him for a couple of hours before admitting him to the hospital for overnight observation.

There was another interesting case that happened at that hospital. One Saturday night a car arrived at the ER with a man who had been shot through the right side of his chest. The bullet had gone completely through the chest, as indicated by the exit wound to the back. Along with all the other supportive care that was rendered, a STAT chest X-ray was done which revealed a pneumothorax, which was what Joe had suspected. Dr. Joe put in a chest tube to suction and the nurses were getting him ready for the ICU when the man who had shot him showed up at the Emergency Room with a pistol to finish him off. There was no hospital security in those days because these type things had never happened. But they did that night. Before the shooter could get into the examining room to shoot the victim again, the Radiology Technician, who was a big guy himself, grabbed him, took the gun away and wrestled him to the floor where he held him until the police arrived.

AIR GUARD BUSINESS

D r. Joe's best friend was, again, the commander of the Air Guard in Meridian and so it seemed all was well with the guard. On one flight the Colonel had also been the victim of a buzzard coming through the quarter panel of the F-4 jet he was flying only a year before. He was struck on the left shoulder at 500 ft. altitude while flying at a speed of 480 knots, that's about 535 miles per hour, on a low level mission, sustaining a fracture of the left shoulder. He was not too far away from Egland AFB, LA, so he and the back seater, who was also an instructor pilot, were able to get the aircraft on the ground without further injury.

But, in the U.S. Air Force if you are a pilot on flight status, you must have a flight physical once a year. The Commander came in and Joe did his annual flight physical and all appeared normal. Dr. Joe had an EKG done on him, as was the rule. Joe looked at the EKG and it appeared normal, but he was also required to send it to Lackland AFB, San Antonio, Texas for an over read. Unfortunately the reader at Lackland saw a flaw in the EKG. The Colonel was sent for further evaluation and unfortunately, in the long run, he required bypass surgery. He was permanently grounded and discharged on permanent disability. This ended Dr. Joe's old friend's career in the military service. Joe felt terrible about this for years, but there was nothing he could have done differently.

Chapter 7
The Panama Mission

THERE WAS, IN 1980, a very important mission for the Air Guard to fly to what is now The Republic of Panama. But before we get into that, some review of history regarding how and why the U.S. government became involved in Panama is necessary.

Panama had originally been a Spanish possession in the 16th century and was originally discovered by Balboa. The importance of the Isthmus of Panama became obvious early on by the Spaniards when they were faced with the chore of getting their goods across a 50 mile stretch of land to the Pacific Ocean in order to trade with the Asian countries; or go by boat all the way around the Cape of Chile, which required a long haul and a lot of time in those days.

In the late 19th century, a French engineer by the name of Ferdinand de Lesseps was able to get a grant of 5 billion dollars to build that long thought out and awaited Panama Canal. However he was to have extreme cost overruns and tropical diseases, including malaria, which would prove to be the undoing of the project, along with the disruptive corrupt politics in France that caused him to give up the project.

The United States, however, had been interested from the beginning in wanting the canal; but had first decided to build a canal through Nicaragua. However, with the French failure in Panama, the time and situation was ripe for the U.S. to move in and complete the canal. But the Colombian government, which had held sovereignty over the canal, did not really want the U.S. to build it.

Another French engineer, Philippe-Jean Bunau-Varilla, also had a large stake in the canal and only stood to avert financial disaster if the U.S. would come in and finish the canal. By now the U.S. had much unused power, money and badly needed equipment. Finally after much wrangling, along with the fact that the Panamanian people were asserting their independence from Colombia, the U.S. Congress passed the Hay-Bauno-Varilla treaty which did two things. It guaranteed Panama's independence from Colombia and committed the U.S. to build the canal. However, the Colombians were not so happy about all this; so the U.S. ended up sending gunboats to the canal area to be certain that things would go as planned.

It was at this time that it was realized that yellow fever and malaria were spread by mosquitos. At that point much of the effort was to control the mosquito population. And control of the mosquito population did lessen the number of cases of disease.

Although Ferdinand de Lesseps dug the Suez Canal, he realized that this was a totally different project because he was not digging through sand. It was rock he was digging through, not to mention that the water level of the ocean was 110 meters below the lowest point of the terrain. Also the Chagres River crossed the proposed canal in the Colon portion of the route. Its channel would need to be diverted to the ocean short of the canal.

De Lesseps, as project engineer, estimated it would take an excavation of 120,000,000 million tons of dirt and rock at a cost of $120.000,000. He estimated the canal would be 29.5 feet deep at water level and 72 feet wide. On May 15, 1889 the project went bankrupt with the canal two-fifths finished. This was prior to the U.S. becoming involved in the project.

On May 4th, 1904 Lt. Jatara O'Neil of the U.S. army was presented the keys to the canal. The Canal Zone was overseen by a special commission called the Isthmian Canal Commission. The canal was far from functional at this time. It was not yet decided whether it should be a sea level or a lock canal. Finally, President Roosevelt and the U.S. Congress agreed on a lock canal. After much debate and bureaucratic delay it was decided that the Army Corp of Engineers would finish building the canal.

One of the greatest barriers to this whole project was cutting through the Culebra or what extended as far south as the remnant of what we know as the Continental Divide (which is part of what formed the Rocky Mountains in the western U.S.) One might not think about the big divide extending this far south, but it does. And if one were traveling from New York to San Francisco one would save 7800 sea miles of travel by going through the canal at Panama.

Dynamite was used to blast the rock and finally more than 99 million cubic yards of rock was removed from the site. The locks were finally finished in 1911 and 1913. And the canal was finally finished and operational on April 1, 1914 and the keys were handed over to the canal authority.

Worth quoting: From the Rotunda of the Panama Canal Administration Bldg.

"IT IS NOT THE CRITIC that counts, not the man who points out how the strong man stumbled, or where the doer of deeds could have done them better. The credit belongs to the man who is actually in the arena; whose face is marred by dust and sweat and blood; who strives valiantly, who errs and comes up short again and again; who knows the great enthusiasms, the great devotions and spends himself in a worthy cause; who, at best knows in the end the triumph of high achievement; and who, at worst, if he fails, at least fails while daring greatly, so that his place shall never be with those cold and timid souls who know neither victory nor defeat."

AT THE TIME OF COMPLETION of the canal the world was now preoccupied with the coming of WWI, so attention was then redirected at the great challenges now put before the world community.

There have since been added two more sets of locks, one of which is large enough to handle the super tanker sized ships. In 1977 President Jimmy Carter decided that the control of the locks and the Canal Zone should be turned over to the Panamanians. Why he took that action is still a mystery, but maybe it's not so strange when considering his thinking on other issues. Control of the canal has been a matter of political controversy ever since.

Knowing the actual history of the canal and its construction is enough to understand why it has always been incumbent on the U.S. to defend, at all costs, the continued operation and safety of the Canal Zone area. Having established that much, it is not too farfetched to realize why a flight of four RF4s was sent from the Meridian Air Guard to the Canal Zone in January of 1980 to shoot a mosaic photography of the whole area. Dr. Joe was at that time a flight surgeon in the 153rd Tac Recon Squadron with the Meridian Mississippi Air National Guard and was privileged to be in one of the four aircraft in the flight. They took off from Key Field in Meridian on a cold morning in January and intercepted the refueling tankers just south of New Orleans for a top off on fuel, then headed immediately south towards Panama. They landed at the Tocumen Air Field where they would be based for the next week. Colonel Noriega was in charge of the Panamanian government at that time and there were numerous complaints through the halls of the U.S. government that Noriega was running a drug operation into the United States and the task was to try to canvas the area from the air by photography to find if there was any evidence of drug running. However, the crew had been told in advance that they were not to fly immediately over his home.

Upon landing, the crews were taken by bus to the officer's quarters where they unloaded their gear. The quarters were nice enough. Everyone got their showers and then dressed for the cocktail hour at the officer's club. When Joe entered the club and went to the bar he noticed the clientele at the bar was a mixture of the strangest variation of people that he had ever seen. It seemed to be a mixture of every race and every nationality. They were standing in small groups and there was hardly any standing room left. And they were talking in different tongues. Some were in uniform and some were not. He did hear one of them ask another whether his shipment of "stuff" had come in from Colombia. To which the other one said, "Yes. I will send it on up through the usual route to the U.S." Joe assumed they must have been talking drugs.

Joe was standing there having a drink with his guard buddies when he felt a hand on his shoulder from behind. He turned around and to his surprise who was it? None but one Cody Redwine from Great Falls, Montana, who had been the lead groomsman in his wedding. It had been several years since they had seen each other. Joe explained to Cody that the Mississippi Air Guard was down there on a special investigative mission to do a mosaic photo run on the whole Canal Zone. The U.S. government, along with a whole lot of other people, were concerned about the landslide of illicit drugs that was coming through the Canal Zone. Addiction levels and death rates in the U.S. were at all time highs because of the illicit drugs getting through to the U.S. Both these guys had Top Secret clearances so they were not talking out of school.

Cody said he had been recruited by the DEA (Drug Enforcement Administration) to penetrate the drug network of first Columbia and Bolivia, and then Peru to try to establish where exactly the drugs were coming from, as well as how and to whom they were being shipped, and the method of shipment. Cody went on to say that the DEA was furnishing him a special small two man helicopter with which to do his interdictive work. They also wanted it to be a two man operation but up to this time they had not recruited the second guy. He asked, "Joe, would you be interested in being that second guy? I've been thinking a lot about you lately but it has not been convenient to ask. You know we go way back to the Bay of Pigs and I don't think there is anyone I know better or would rather go in there with than you." Joe said, "Hey man, thanks. It sounds like something we could do, but I would need to talk to Lisa before I committed to anything like that. You know, I'm a family man with four kids now."

Cody said he understood, then went on to say that the DEA had supplied a specially built super quiet helicopter designed for the mission. They would locate, through intelligence, approximately where the operators of the drug lords hang out and where and how they do their work. "It will be an exceedingly daring and dangerous mission but we both know what that's all about. We've been there before. What do you say?" Joe said, "Cody, you really know how to rattle my cage don't you?" They both laughed, and then Joe said, "I will talk to Lisa. You know me well enough to know that there is no one I would rather fight back to back with than you. We *have* been there before. I will talk to Lisa as soon as I get back home and let you know." Cody nodded, "We would make the perfect team. The mission would take from 3 to 6 months, depending on how rapidly we could find the information that the DEA is wanting." Joe asked, "How can I contact you after I talk with Lisa?" Cody gave him a contact number. They then returned to the bar and joined Joe's fellow crewmen from the Air Guard. Joe explained to them that he and Cody were old friends who had participated in the failed attempt by the CIA to retake Cuba from Castro. They accepted him as the true patriot that he was. They then all retired to the dining room where they had more drinks and dinner. After that everyone said good night and returned to the officer's quarters.

The next day Joe and the rest of the flight flew their first operational missions. Each of the four crews had specifically designed areas and targets to shoot from the air. They would return after the missions and download their photo coverage of the areas they were tasked to shoot. Joe's crew of two was specifically tasked to shoot a mosaic film of the complete western coast of Panama all the way up to the Costa Rican line and back down the western side to the Colombian line. This they did without incident. In the next several days they would continue shooting pictures of specific areas that U.S. intelligence was interested in. Even though they had been told not to shoot pictures of Noriega's home, they did anyway. Within 4 or 5 days their mission was complete and they were ready to travel home.

All planes again took off headed north and soon after takeoff they hit the refueling tanker for a fuel top off and they were then off and running. The trip home would take about two and a half hours. All landed safely back at Key Field in Meridian, MS on Sunday afternoon about 1300 hours. The families were there to meet them and Joe was glad to see Lisa and the kids.

That Sunday evening Joe and Lisa were sitting on the couch watching TV when Joe mentioned having seen Cody Redwine while in Panama. He told her about Cody's mission to South America and that Cody had asked Joe if he could come on board with him and that he had told Cody that he would talk to her about it. She said, "Do you really want to go?" Joe took a deep breath and swallowed and said, "Well it would only take between 3 and 6 months and I think that it would be a great contribution to the country in this time of need." Lisa began to tear up and she said, *"You know, Joe, when I met you I knew you were a warrior and a patriot; and even though the very thought of losing you terrifies me, I would not want to stand in your way. You know I have waited for your return before and you have to know it takes a strong woman to say **'Do what you have to do, I'll be right here waiting for you when you return home'.**"*

Joe called Cody the next day to sign on for the mission. Cody was ecstatic. Dr. Joe would leave in one week and meet Cody in Panama and from there they would fly to Bogata, Columbia. Joe took a 6 month leave of absence from his post as Flight Surgeon in the 153rd

Tac Recon Squadron and his hospital responsibilities. They would center their operation in the DEA hanger at Tocumen Air Base in Panama.

Chapter 8
DEA South American Mission

A DEA AIRCRAFT WOULD pick Dr. Joe up at the Meridian Airport, Key Field, Mississippi and transport him directly to the airport in Panama City, Panama and there he would hook up with Cody Redwine and they would fly the mission as assigned by the DEA.

When Joe arrived at the airport in Panama City, Cody was there to meet him. They went to the officer's quarters where Joe deposited the one bag he was carrying and then they were off to the officer's club to eat. While they were eating they were discussing the mission they had been sent there to do privately. Cody said that their purpose there was to investigate what drugs and how much was being produced in Colombia. Finally the DEA wanted to know how the drugs were being transported and who took delivery. The DEA already knew that there was a great transition going on within the drug industry itself. They wanted the same information for Brazil, Bolivia and Peru.

DEA BRIEFING

Joe and Cody received a lengthy and in depth briefing. There was much that was already known about what they should expect from the mission they were about to undertake, but there were also lengthy questions about what the briefer, Manual Acosta, did not know and what the DEA hoped they could discover. In other words it was an open book and they were encouraged to go after details that even the briefer didn't know. For example, even though the U.S. owned the air and seas, billions of dollars in drugs, and in particular cocaine, were getting through to the U.S. The briefer went on to say that this was most disconcerting considering the amount of money already being spent and the cost in terms of money, medical care and lives was quite remarkable. So, he said, it was obvious that there were questions that were unanswered and they didn't even know if they know all the questions concerning how these drugs were getting into the U.S.

The briefer also made special mention of Pablo Escobar who was now the new King Pin Drug Lord of South America. He was now responsible for 80% of the cocaine being consumed worldwide. They needed to know more about him, his operation, how he gets his money and exactly where and how he operates. Then he stated, "It is impossible to over emphasize this part of your mission. This is your mission. We will help you in any way we can and we also are keenly aware of the risk you are undertaking. Your mission is so top secret that not even the top of our own intelligence network or any members of Congress know what you are doing.

You two have been selected because you are the two best people we have. We will assist you in any way we can but where you are going is so remote that we can't even acknowledge that you are part of us without compromising your personal safety. If however we are called upon to rescue you we will do so, even compromising our own safety if necessary. Questions?" Neither Cody nor Joe replied.

"You may assume that you have four countries to investigate, Brazil, Bolivia, Peru, and Columbia. But you are to go where the evidence leads you. You will have a radio in your possession which will reach us without problem. As you already know however, if we can hear you, so can others. So, unless you need to contact us, radio silence is the best policy."

Joe and Cody decided after leaving the officer's club that they would refuel as they were passing through Colombia and try for making it all the way to Brazilian airspace by sunset the following day. They would look for and find an open area under the stars to put the copter down for the night. As they passed through their route through Colombia they noticed a lot of coca fields around the Medellín area of which they were already aware from intelligence reports they had seen. They also knew that this was the home of Pablo Escobar and it only made sense that there would be large amounts of coca in the area. Joe was taking photos as they went through the area and looking for ways to canvas the area when they came back through on the way back to the Canal Zone. They didn't crawl into the sleeping bags until just before dark.

The biggest drug in the past had been marijuana but the drug culture was in the process of switching to the new drug called cocaine. It was an easy plant to grow and the profit margins were extremely high by comparison. The drug industry evolved from a suitcase of marijuana to a relatively small amount of cocaine which would fetch far more money than the marijuana. One kilo of cocaine could bring as high as $50,000. The DEA also wanted to know the details as to how the cartels were making the drugs. Their job was to go to the sources and get any and all information they could on how these operations functioned.

The operation was conducted in absolute secrecy so they would pick up the helicopter here in Panama, along with weapons with silencers because if they were detected and caught they would likely to be summarily executed on the spot; so you must be able to defend yourself in a crunch. Also they were to find out how the drugs were being shipped and to whom and in what amounts. And the DEA did not want them to return to Bogota for fueling. There were a number of locations in the jungles where there was fuel. They could spot those fuel points from the air then land and refuel.

They knew they had their work cut out for them. They also had instructions as to whom to see or call in Bogota if needed. The drug areas in question were clearly marked on the maps they were given at their briefing. They were both fluent in the language spoken by the natives. They could take as much time as they needed to conduct the investigation and then when they had completed their mission they would return here to Panama City for debriefing. If at any time during the mission they felt compromised they would kill if necessary. Both had 22 pistols with silencers and AR15s, also with silencers, and knives for hand to hand combat should a confrontation be necessary. They had a map drawn up by the DEA with the areas already known and some other areas that were suspect. They should pay particular attention to these areas and look for trails and roads leading to areas that looked like depots. They already knew the stuff had to go by land through Panama, by sea, or by air, or all of the above. The question was which, how much and when?

They also knew there was a relatively new kid on the block who was as lethal as he was effective in deliverance of drugs. His name was Pablo Escobar, whose home base was northwest from Bogata. So this is where their marching orders began.

Some background on the cocaine business is in order. The small rural community of Rionegro, near Medellin has the distinction of being the birth place of Pablo Escobar on Dec 2, 1949. He was the third of seven children born to a farmer. He grew up in Medellin where he attended the university but never graduated. His criminal life began there by doing street scams such as selling bogus diplomas for university graduation and bogus lottery tickets. So drug selling did not corrupt him, he was corrupt from the beginning. Later he would capture important business men and hold them for ransom. Marijuana was on its way out because there was not enough profit potential compared to the new upcoming drug cocaine. He was able to secure a small amount of cocaine paste and from there his business and his notoriety began. By the time he was 27 years old he had already banked in excess of 3 million U.S. dollars. But this was just the start.

By the early 1980's Pablo Escobar would just be starting to build a drug trafficking operation that would exceed the wildest expectations of even those involved since. There were no cartels at the time, that is, no wide distribution networks. So Pablo saw a future with a potential that was unlimited. He would go on to set up a cartel empire that would rival and exceed any other of all time.

Pablo knew that all he had to do was get the cocaine by the U.S. border guards and into the hands of a few users and he would not be able too meet the demand. First he knew the way to start would be delivery by land. That would be the simplest, quickest way; but he would be limited to getting it by the customs agents of the countries he had to cross. And one of the main players in this would be General Noriega of Panama.

He knew that he could either go through Mexico or bypass it by water or air to get his product to the United States. The key was to organize smuggling routes to South Florida and Southern California. Escobar even acquired the use of a privately owned island in the Bahamas and put in a 3500 foot landing strip to use as a drop off point. Estimates of the amount of shipments in the early eighties were that more than 70 tons per month were being shipped. And this was the specific reason that reconnaissance missions such as this by Cody and Joe were necessary. Thus Cody and Joe departed Panama heading to Columbia on their highly secret mission for the DEA.

Cody and Joe knew there would be less activity around the growth areas farthest from Medellin, or at least that was their judgement call, so they decided to over fly the northern sector nearest Medellin and start in the southern portions of the country. They stopped at one of the secret fueling areas on the way into the country and topped off the fuel. Then they climbed to 3000 feet and headed toward the southern part of the country and the most southern patch of coca plants indicated on their map. That would be the area called Putumayo Caquetá. It was an area south and east of Cali.

As they approached the southeastern corner of this patch they could see clearly with the binoculars that this was one of the patches they had seen on photos from the air. Cody was flying and he flew so as to circumnavigate the area from the left so that they might case the area for activity before attempting to land. In the process they did locate the processing area and a road leading into the processing area. They saw no vehicles or personnel on the ground so they landed in a spot that was clear of the processing area by about 100 yards. Cody shut down the engine and they got out and carefully made their way to the processing area. In flying around the plot they thought there were several hundred acres in this relatively small part of the operation but the photos Joe had shot on the way in would reveal exactly how much acreage was involved here.

They had been taught all the stages of processing the coca and there were a number of large vats around the area, some full of leaves and liquid and others indicating that these different vats were at different stages of making cocaine. They took pictures of all the vats and the whole operation and were about to depart when they heard a vehicle approaching. They had been briefed to avoid detection and confrontation at all cost, so they hustled on back to the helicopter and got out before they were detected or at least as far as they could tell. While there Joe had shot pictures of everything including a stack of papers that were lying on the table. These would later prove to be instructions for processing and some also having to do with where this cocaine would be sent.

Having left apparently undetected, their next stop would be Meta Guaviare, a hundred or so miles northeast of their present position. However, night was beginning to come upon them and they needed a place to stop until daybreak. They found what they thought was a very remote location not too far from their next target area and Cody put the copter down and shut down the engine. The DEA had put special noise abaters on this aircraft to purposely cause as little engine and rotor noise as possible. They pulled out their sleeping bags and crawled in for the night.

The next morning they ate some of the military meals that had been sent with them and drank from their supply of fresh drinking water. It was a low seventies morning and very humid and the jungle around them looked daunting. They stuck to the plan and by 0800 hrs they were airborne and headed for the next coca patch. It was another huge plot a hundred miles or so from where they had visited yesterday. They used the same procedure of flying the perimeter first and then getting closer for a second look before going in for an in depth inspection. As one might expect though, there was early morning activity at this one. They decided to fly off out of distance and wait for a time and then check back in a couple of hours. They landed in a vacant field well out of sight of any roads or activity and waited for two hours.

Then they got back in the copter and retraced their flight back to the coca patch and this time no one was in sight. They proceeded to land about 100 yards away and shut down the machine. They made their way to the processing sight and were in the process of taking inventory of the sight when a truck rapidly approached from nowhere. This was not a case of not being careful; it was just that they could not hear the truck until it was on top of them. They were both stunned by the suddenness of the developing scene. Both of these guys were experienced and knew how to fight and they knew they had been discovered by hostile forces. No one had to tell them to draw their weapons and fire at will. There were three men that bailed out of the truck. They killed all three of them and quietly went about their business of inventory of the site complete with photos of everything. That done, they departed quickly for the copter and were airborne in 30 seconds.

The next stop would be Arauca on the Colombian-Venezuelan border. Before they could arrive though night was falling again. They landed just barely on the Colombian side of the border in a remote area. They were careful not to use any form of light. As part of their gear though they did carry night goggles in case they were needed. Early the next morning they would carry out the 3rd leg of their mission. In the meantime they got some shut eye.

This was a fairly small area by comparison to some of the areas they had already worked. They decided to wait where they were until the noon hour before they went in for their inspection. At 1200 hrs they loaded up the copter and flew the short distance in towards the site. As they had hoped everyone was gone so they landed about 100 yards from the site, shut down the engine and walked to the site. It was by comparison a smaller operation than the others they had inspected, although very revealing. There were the usual vats in various stages of the filtering process. Joe was going through the paperwork he found on one of the tables and taking photos when he looked in detail at what was written in Spanish. The paper was addressed to General Noriega, and it was at that moment that the parts of the puzzle began to come together. Joe said to Cody, "Noriega is the Kingpin in a smuggling operation through Panama. Apparently Panama is the lynch pin or jumping off point of the world's biggest drug smuggling ring. The DEA will be happy to know this. I have all the papers and photos so lets get out of here while the getting is still good." With that they quickly made their way back to the helicopter and were shortly airborne.

By now it was about 1500 hours and they still had a while before dark so they headed just north to an area called Norte de Santander hoping to get there after the workers had left for the day. This plot was about 100 miles straight north and also right on the Venezuelan border so it took only about an hour to get there. They arrived and as usual they cased the joint from the air and seeing no one they landed about 100 yards away. There were several hundred acres of plants of which Joe took moving pictures as they circled. There was nothing here that they had not already seen but just the same they looked at and took pictures of everything. And in looking at the papers, Joe saw once again that the labels showed that the stuff was going directly to General Noriega. They made their way back to the copter loaded up and headed out.

The next plot was the one located about 10 miles north of the city of Medellin, the headquarters of the now budding Cartel of Pablo Escobar. He was the new budding Czar of the cocaine drug cartel according to the intelligence reports they had heard. They were flying on a southwesterly heading from their last stop but it was about to get dark so they decided to stop for the night and attack this one tomorrow at the noon hour. Why noon? Because that would likely be the time that no one would be there. So they landed in an isolated area and quietly bedded down for the night. They were tired so they stayed in their sleeping bags until about 0900 hours and slowly began to stir about. They ate some of their rations and Cody remarked, "This doesn't taste all that bad. I've eaten worse at a Mexican honky-tonk." While continuing with the small talk Cody said, "How is Lisa?" To which Joe replied, "She and the kids are only things I really miss on this trip. I'm looking forward to getting home to them. You know the most fun of any trip is getting home again."

By now it was noon, so they made their preparations for leaving and loaded up the gear. It was 1210 hrs. so it was time to move in to the Medellin plot. After this run they would take a look over in Peru, Bolivia and Brazil. They knew there were similar operations there but the details they did not know and that's why they needed to take a look at those places as well.

By now they were approaching the huge field of coca plants from the north and this was one of the largest they had seen. As they approached from the north at about 400 feet they could see that this was no small operation. It appeared from the air to cover some 1000-1200 acres and they could see the processing plant at about the middle of the huge rectangular plot. They scouted the whole area before landing in the plot about 100 yards from the processing area. Once on the site the saw that this was more of the same, only larger and they also noted that there was a machine designed to smash or cut the leaves into smaller parts. This was obviously to make it easier and quicker to extract the coca from the leaves. Joe took pictures of everything and again all the papers. He took particular note again that the finished product would be going to General Noriega in Panama. Just as they were finishing they found that they had been discovered, because a pickup truck was rapidly approaching on the road. There were two men riding in the cab and 4 in the bed of the pickup.

They made their way quickly to the helicopter, but were too late to make it out without a fight. As the men piled out of the pickup, Joe and Cody shot and killed all six of them. What they had not counted on though was that there were two armed guards at each corner of the field, a total of eight who were making rapid advances towards them while firing their AK47s at them. These guys must have been under camouflage because they should have seen them on the way in. Cody took on the four on his side and Joe took on the four coming from his side. Joe killed all four on his side and Cody killed three on his side but the last one hit Cody in the right shoulder knocking him to the ground. Joe whirled around to Cody's side in time to shoot the last one down. The pair then ran as fast as they could to the copter. Joe threw the AR15s into the copter and helped Cody into his seat, jumped in and started the engine. Joe gave it full power and with maximum blade angle they lifted off to the north. But not before yet another truck load of hombres arrived and were shooting at them as they departed. One bullet pierced the windshield and another struck the left landing gear. Nothing was hit that would keep the aircraft from flying. Joe put the aircraft in a max climb toward the north before he had time to assess Cody's shoulder wound. Dr. Joe noted that the entry point was just above the right clavicle and there was an exit wound through the trapezius muscle posteriorly. It did not appear to hit the scapula and there was no evidence that there was a pneumothorax.

They headed north to Panama and leveled off at 3500 feet. They had plenty of gas to get back and as soon as they were able to receive the Panama Vortac they tracked right in from the south. As soon as Joe was within 25 miles of the Panama Airport he called the tower, told them the situation and got clearance to land right in front of the DEA hanger. He also requested that an ambulance meet them to pick up the wounded man.

After landing and shutting down the engine, the ambulance was there immediately and took Cody to the hospital. Joe, meanwhile, went into the DEA hanger and delivered his briefing to the DEA. The DEA had long suspected that Noriega was a big player in the drug smuggling of cocaine and now they had the proof. But now came the part of the puzzle as to how Noriega was moving the drugs to North America. These were the next questions to be answered in stopping the flow of drugs that were killing Americans. As a matter of completeness there was also the lingering question of the involvement of Brazil, Peru and Bolivia. But this would be another day and another mission. First they had to get Cody healed and then they could talk about future missions.

Now Pablo Escobar was just beginning his rise to prominence as the world's Kingpin of cocaine makers and distributors. As early as 1976 Pablo had bought cocaine paste from a source in Peru. And as the first cocaine arrived in the U.S. the demand for it expectedly sky rocketed. Pablo and his lifelong friend Carlos Lehder worked together to establish supply routes in the Bahamas which would supply both the U.S. and Europe. Lehder even bought an island in the Bahamas which had a landing strip. The island was a complete processing and shipping center for cocaine. Indeed Pablo had come a long way from the days of shipping by mule, as it was called. Those were the days when marijuana was shipped in the suitcases of flight attendants.

Finally, Pablo wanted respectability as well, so he had himself elected to the Chamber of Representatives of Colombia. Also the production process was moved mainly to Bolivia and Peru where the cocaine production process was even more fine tuned. As Pablo became more of a menace to the U.S. and other countries, the U.S. began to work with the Colombian government to change the extradition process of Colombia so that Pablo could be extradited and tried in the United States. In retaliation the group called MS19 broke into government buildings and burned all papers having to do with extradition. Hostages were also taken and their release was negotiated. But Pablo Escobar was seen by the locals as a hero. He gave liberally of his money to causes of the people that he felt worthy. He was a folk hero.

Joe had shared all the information that had been gained on their mission to Columbia with the DEA in debriefing and it apparently filled in many of the blanks they had been looking for. They had long suspected Noriega's involvement, but now they had firm evidence. The question was exactly how they were getting the drugs through Mexico and whether some of it was being flown in and if some of it was being shipped by water, and if so, how and when.

Dr. Joe's initial assessment of Cody's injury proved to be essentially correct in that he received no serious injury from his gunshot wound in their last confrontation in Colombia and now 2 weeks later he was completely healed and ready for duty. So Joe picked up Cody at the hospital where he had been treated and released. They went to the officer's club and sat down for a one-on-one as to what they thought their next move would be. They knew their mission wasn't finished. There was still the matter of the coca leaf labs in Brazil, Peru and Bolivia. Coca was nothing new to these two countries. Their farmers frequently chewed dry coca leaves while working in the fields to give them that added burst of energy to finish the day strong. Those coca farmers might look at you and say, "Well, what's the big deal?" Anyway all this in Brazil, Peru and Bolivia needed to be looked into. So Joe looked at Cody and said, "Do we want to finish what we started or do we want to quit and go home?" To which Cody quickly answered, "Quit and go home without finishing the mission? Hell no!" So Joe and Cody set up a meeting with the DEA at the DEA hanger briefing room for the next morning.

At the meeting the new DEA briefer, Joel DeCosta, laid out the case plain and simple. He said, "You have been enormously successful in the first mission. You have provided us with most of the information we need. However, we would like to know the kind and extent of the operations in Brazil, Bolivia and Peru. We do have information which makes us think that those two operations in Bolivia and Peru are now making the most sophisticated cocaine to date. It is high potency and there are many new deaths being attributed to it and we would like to know what they are doing differently in the manufacture of the drug. We have given you the newest, updated helicopter for this mission. We have added more silencer to the engine, but it is more powerful than the last one. And it has a special supercharged engine specifically for high altitude mountainous flying. It has a bulletproof windshield and there is more armament around the engine to deflect enemy ground fire. It has special blades that are bullet resistant but lighter as well. As before you have night vision goggles, but we think by now you are experienced enough with the area and situation that you know how to protect yourselves. Just remember that always, in clandestine operations such as this, the best policy is not to be discovered. There are, again, several secret refueling points along your route, and there are a number of them in Brazil, Peru and Bolivia. Take note of those. You have a complete set of sectional maps in your possession. How did you find your food rations on your last mission?" Joe laughed and said, "Okay when you consider the source." DeCosta smiled, acknowledging Joe's meaning, and said, "Are there further questions? If not, you are on your own as to planning your departure time and route."

They went to the officer's club that evening for dinner and drinks. Cody said, "It's going to be quite a haul down there." Joe said, "Yes, but where we are now is probably the best and most secret spot we could have to begin with. No one would expect us to come there from here. We'd better get out of here and get some sleep, then head for Brazil in the morning.

Joe and Cody were up a the crack of dawn the next morning and at the helicopter in front of the DEA hanger. They carefully went through their checklist of items that had been provided for the mission. This would be the last chance to be sure they had such items as silencers for the pistols they carried, special binoculars and night vision glasses, rations and drinking water.

They then strapped into the copter and Joe called the tower for traffic instructions as Cody lifted the aircraft off the ground. They rose immediately above the hangers and picked up a heading of south as they departed the airport. Joe bade the control tower good day as they climbed on a southerly heading to an altitude of 5000 ft. Soon they were flying over the Darien Gap and as they flew further south they were overflying the eastern edge of Colombia. They continued their southerly heading skirting the western edge of Venezuela. By the end of the day they stopped at one of their secret fuel stops where they topped off the fuel tank. They were almost in Brazil and it appeared they would be near their first overnight stop. About 30 minutes later they arrived in an area that was near the start of the Greater Amazon River Basin. They found an area that appeared to be secluded enough; so they put the copter down in a clear area that was close to the area of interest. They pulled out the sleeping bags and bedded down for the night.

MISSION TO BRAZIL

Joe and Cody were awake at the crack of dawn. They ate and then cleaned up the campsite. Before they boarded the copter though they got out their maps and took a look at the vast expanse of the Amazon jungle and the confluence of the rivers and streams that made up this huge Amazon basin.

What they decided to do was to look for beaten paths through the jungle that obviously would emerge at the water's edge of these rivers. If they were able to do so, surely they would be able to connect the dots to some life forms that were moving up and down the rivers. So they would follow the streams and rivers as they converged until they discovered how the cocaine was being transported and locate the destination.

With this in mind they loaded up in the copter and headed in a generally southeasterly direction until they picked up on what appeared to be a regularly traveled path through the jungle. They continued their heading in a southeasterly direction until it ended at a river, which Joe identified as the Putumayo River, that eventually runs into the Amazon River. Joe remarked to Cody that he didn't ever remember seeing so many rivers and streams running in the same general direction. The trail they had been following ran out at the river so it was obvious that this river, the Putumayo, was being used for transportation of the drugs.

They decided to follow the Putumayo to the Amazon to see if, in fact, there was any traffic on the water. They had gone about 25 miles down the river when they noticed a boat up ahead that was going the same direction they were headed. Cody slowed the copter and stayed a safe distance behind, while Joe took pictures of the boat and the surrounding area. They noticed that there were some containers sitting near the center of the boat which looked to be about two feet square. There were two men in the boat and they were traveling about 20 miles per hour. Joe said to Cody, "Wonder what's in those boxes." Cody laughed and replied, "Just no telling." Meanwhile Joe was shooting a mosaic picture tour. Joe and Cody decided that they would move on downstream for now to see how close they were to the Amazon. They would see if there was a planned rendezvous for this boat and another further downstream.

With the information they now had, they flew on downstream until the Putumayo joined the Amazon. There they stopped and put the aircraft down in a clear spot close to the junction of the two rivers and took a rest and planning break. After they were out of the aircraft Cody said he thought that was cocaine on that boat. To which Joe said, "I agree." Joe continued, "I think we are in a good spot here to walk the 50 yards to the river and watch for them to pass. I would think their plan is to rendezvous with another boat at some pickup point and off-load their cargo."

With all this in mind they found a secure spot along the river's edge and waited. They knew about how fast the boat was traveling so they leisurely waited for the boat to make its appearance. It was now approaching four in the afternoon and according to their calculation that boat should be arriving within the next few minutes. Sure enough about 6 minutes later the boat made its appearance and passed them without being aware that they were being watched. Joe and Cody waited a few minutes after the boat had passed and then made their way back to the aircraft.

In moments they were off and flying down the Amazon, which, after being joined by the Putumayo, was now a much larger body of water. It wasn't long before they spotted the boat ahead. By now it was late afternoon when they noticed a larger boat approaching from the east coming up the Amazon river. Before they hardly knew it the two boats stopped close to each other. Cody and Joe kept their distance so that maybe the smugglers wouldn't see their aircraft while they watched them unload the cargo from the smaller boat to the larger boat. They were beginning to put the puzzle together now. This was probably part of a regular cargo run made by these boats.

Once the cargo was loaded onto the larger boat, the smaller boat reversed its course and started back up the river towards Joe and Cody. At that point Cody moved the craft out over the jungle enough not to be seen. Then Cody move the aircraft downstream so they could see which direction the larger boat had gone. As it turned out the larger pickup boat started moving upstream. Putting two and two together, Joe and Cody surmised that this larger boat had more than one pickup point. They followed the boat, staying far enough behind that with the camouflaging paint of their aircraft they could follow but not be seen. They followed the boat upstream for about another 10 miles where the boat pulled alongside another smaller boat and again took on a number of boxes. By now Joe and Cody knew they had discovered a regular cocaine run. Once the larger boat had taken on its load, it reversed course and headed back downstream.

Joe and Cody followed the boat back down the Amazon for about another twenty miles where it pulled into a pier and appeared to be docking for the night. Joe and Cody found a small clearing in the jungle and put the copter down for the night. They found a spot right next to the copter and sat down and ate their rations. They put their sleeping bags on the ground and prepared to bed down. They were beginning to hear the night creatures sing but otherwise it was quiet. Their sleeping bags were right next to a big tree. They were both sitting on their sleeping bags when something fell from the tree hitting Cody on the back. At that moment, Joe and Cody saw that it was a snake, and a fairly large one. Cody quickly moved away from it and grabbed a stick and killed the snake. After this paralyzing incident was over they identified the snake as a Forest Pit Viper, a very poisonous viper that climbs trees and is known to spring from trees onto its victim. There are other pit vipers in the Amazon forest but this one is the only one known to climb trees. Joe and Cody zipped themselves up tight in the sleeping bags for the night.

They were awake at first dawn and they could hear activity down the river where the boat had parked last evening. Apparently the boat was departing for other places. They got into the copter and headed down river and soon they could see the boat ahead of them. It was running about 20 mph headed to the east so they just kept the boat in sight. As they were flying along, Joe suddenly noticed on the south side of the river a fairly large patch of coca plants. They decided to land and pretend to be coca buyers. There was a covered area close by and they noticed that one man was there at the site. Cody put the copter down near the area and Joe and Cody walked over for a visit. Cody asked the man in broken Portuguese if he had cocaine for sale. The man said indeed he did but that it was already sold. The man was about 5 ft. 6 inches in height, slim and appeared to be of Indian descent. The man said his name was Ramon Desantes. Cody asked if he knew where the cocaine went from here; to which the man responded, "Buenos Aires." He said, "Some of it is used locally and some of it goes to Africa and Spain." But according to this man much was used by the locals of Brazil, right around the larger cities. Cody asked if they picked up the cocaine by boat and Ramon said yes. But, he said he had heard that some of it was moved by aircraft.

Cody and Joe returned to the copter and flew down river for what seemed to be several hundred miles. Finally they reached a location where there was a large pier and sort of a store and a gas pump. They found an area that was out of sight and put the copter down. The same boat that they had seen upstream was parked at the pier. They felt that they had at least identified a main supply hub for the cocaine from up the river.

The question now was where does it go from here and how does it get there? They made their way to the store and asked the store operator who owned the boat and he said he didn't know. Then Cody asked what the boat was used for and the man replied he didn't know. Joe and Cody knew that the boat was used to haul cocaine down the river. The question was by whom and where are they delivering the cocaine.

The farmer they had spoken with back up the river, said that the boat went up the river about twice a week. So there was only one way to find out where the cocaine was going and that was to sit and wait until the boat made its next run. The surrounding area was sort of a business/nightclub area with several bars and nightclubs located close by. So that night Joe and Cody made the rounds to the night spots and they found plenty of drinking going on and there was some cocaine being sniffed and smoked. They made efforts to befriend other customers and all were nice enough but no one said they knew where the supply of cocaine came from. All of them said it came from friends.

Now we are talking here about the city of Manaus which is the economic hub of the Amazon river and northwestern Brazil. It is another 900 miles downriver to the Atlantic Ocean. Manaus is a city of 2.1 million and Brazil, with a population of 150 million plus, presented a complex problem as to where all this cocaine went. Joe and Cody expected a large amount of it was being used locally. Manaus was a large metropolitan complex which had evolved over time. It had an international airport and a harbor facility that was large enough for ocean going vessels to dock, load and unload.

Manaus is the capital of the state of Amazonas. It was in the 1920's the rubber center of Brazil, but in the late 1920's the rubber industry fell on hard times. Besides the illicit cocaine industry Manaus was also known for its ship building, petroleum refining, manufacture of chemicals and electronics. So what Cody and Joe found themselves embroiled in was a huge metropolis looking for the proverbial needle in the haystack. It was easy for the cocaine industry to just blend into the woodwork. They had now found the regional storage depot for the cocaine but they desperately needed to know where the cocaine went from here and who would get it. Joe and Cody spent two days and nights before the boat made another run up the river. In the meantime they had rented a motor scooter to get around the area.

When the boat went up the river and back the next trip, they watched it as two men, appearing to be Indian, unloaded the boxes off the boat and into a van. There were 10 or 12 boxes in all. The van then departed and they followed on the scooter. It traveled about 2 miles before it turned right and pulled up to a warehouse and stopped. One of the men got out and went through the front door, while the other drove the van around to the rear and pulled it into the warehouse. All this happened while Joe and Cody watched from across the street. After about 5 minutes the van reappeared and was parked in front of the building.

It was getting late in the afternoon and the two men that drove the van again came out of the warehouse and got into their separate cars and left the premises. A short time later another man left the warehouse, presumably the office manager. It appeared that everyone had gone home for the day. So now Joe and Cody knew that this was at least one of the distribution points for the cocaine business in these parts. They noticed before they left that there was a back door to the warehouse. They would return later. They needed to know more about the final destination of the cocaine.

That evening they went up and down the nightclub strip visiting as many bars as possible to listen for tips that might fill in the blanks or connect the dots. There was obviously plenty of cocaine in use though. Finally about midnight Joe and Cody decided it was time to return to the warehouse and see if they could enter and find the information they needed. They got on the scooter and within a few minutes they were approaching the warehouse. They carefully pulled to the rear of the warehouse so that they could not be seen from the street, dismounted and went to the rear door which was out of site of the traffic on the street. They had brought with them a few simple tools, a screwdriver, a knife, a pair of pliers. They also brought a small drill in case they had to gain access to a dead bolt. Cody was especially adept at lock picking.

Within moments he had loosened the locks and they were inside. They carefully closed the door to make it appear that it was still locked. They used subdued light flashlights and began their investigation. They found the boxes of cocaine stacked in several places in the warehouse apparently indicating that different stacks were to be delivered to different places. They looked inside some of the boxes and there were 10 separately wrapped packages of cocaine hydrochloride in each box. The boxes were stacked so they could easily be counted and there 98 boxes total, which would have a street value of at least 700 million dollars. This was no small operation. They then looked at the address labeling on the boxes. Some were going to Rio De Janeiro, some to Casa Blanca on the African continent, some to Spain and some to the Netherlands. So these guys were supplying the African continent, Europe and Spain in addition to the Rio De Janeiro area of Brazil. Now they needed to see the inside of the office complex to look for a list of contacts.

As soon as they approached the door of the office near the front of the building they noted that it was protected by a camera and a door alarm. Cody carefully disconnected the camera, opened it and destroyed the camera. Then they traced the connection to the door alarm and disarmed it. After disarming the alert system they stepped right into the office. By now it was 2:45 am and they needed to find that contact list and move along as rapidly as possible. In one of the desk drawers they found the list and took it with them. They would take pictures of it later. It really didn't matter because as soon as the office manager arrived back at work he would know that someone had broken in during the night anyway.

They had finished their work and were just pulling out onto the street when a police car arrived on the premises apparently making routine rounds. They sped away down the street and back to the pier on the river where they had started this whole long trek. When they arrived at the motor scooter rental facility they left the scooter with the key still in the ignition and faded into the darkness as they made their way back to their helicopter which was parked in a remote area about a mile from the pier. As they arrived back at the chopper, Joe told Cody that he sure wished he had the ability to pick locks. Cody said, "You don't need to as long as you take me along. Besides, I would be dead by now if you hadn't killed those guys in Medellin that shot me through the neck."

They crawled into their sleeping bags and waited for dawn to plot their next move. They were awake not long after their nap started by the roar of jet engines from the international airport, which was several miles away. As they climbed out of their sleeping bags they immediately began accessing their mission thus far and what they should do next. They knew that Bolivia was next on the list but they did notice on the way here that there were some fields of coca plants close to the Brazil-Colombian border in the extreme southern part of Colombia. They decided that they would pay that area a visit before visiting the two large Bolivian sites of which they were already aware.

It was a little over two hours back to the areas in question and when they arrived at the northern most site they circumnavigated the area and noticed there was one farmer attending the site. They landed about 100 yards away and walked over to where the farmer appeared to be busy making paste. He was friendly and they introduced themselves as potential buyers, speaking in Spanish. The farmer said that he had about 45 hector acres, which is about 100 hundred acres American. He was busy making cocaine HCL paste. Joe asked to whom did he sell his paste? He said some times to Pablo but lately someone down river at Manaus had been buying it. Joe and Cody decide it is time to go on to Bolivia.

MISSION TO BOLIVIA

Joe and Cody lifted off at 0700 hrs. the next morning with their sights set on trying to get as far as possible through Brazil and Columbia the first day. It would take them, at 110 knots ground speed about 2 days flying to reach the Bolivian border. They had two areas there to be explored. One was in the northwestern part of the country, Yungas, and Compare in the south central part of the State of Bolivia. They decided that since Peru was the next stop that they would check out Compare in the southern portion of Bolivia first. Their understanding was that the Bolivian people were a generally friendly folk and not prone to fighting.

The following morning they lifted the copter off and headed on towards Bolivia arriving at their predetermined area for camping just before dark. They had skirted along the Brazilian border along the way and had finally crossed into Bolivia where they would look at the coca fields that intelligence had told them about.

They also knew that the Bolivians, especially the rural types, were very friendly towards outsiders, especially Americans. These people generally meant no harm as long as you were friendly to them. They just loved chewing on those dried coca leaves and feeling good about things.

So the next morning they circled their first coca operation and landed near where one local guy was busy working with the processing of the coca. Cody introduce himself and Joe as part of the management. The worker then proceeded to talk the two of them through the whole process of making coca paste. He explained how they beat the leaves until they reduce them into the smallest possible parts of leaves and then added kerosene to separate the coca from the leaves, which involves a filtering process, and then how they added sulfuric acid plus a caustic lime soda to make cocaine sulfate. Then they added kerosene again and filtered out the cocaine paste which is Cocaine HCL, the white powder that can be snorted or shot intravenously. Or they added diluted sulfuric acid and potassium permanganate to make Crack, which is a crystal-like substance that can be smoked and is the most addictive form of the drug.

Cody then asked the worker where their cocaine went once they were through processing it and the worker responded that it was his understanding that their cocaine went to Brazil and Argentina and would go largely to Spain and Holland for distribution to Europe and Asia. Joe and Cody had heard via a drug grapevine that a kilo of cocaine on the street in Spain or Holland went for $40,000, Britain $40,000, Tokyo $100,000 or Russia $80,000. But that was not all, the little Bolivian man also said that some of the acreage in Bolivia was owned by Pablo Escobar, but which acreage or how much he was not sure. Just at that moment Joe and Cody spotted a truck about a mile away headed straight for their location and since they did not know what kind of reception they might get, they quickly made it back to the chopper and headed out.

They were off to the next large patch of coca plants, which according to the intelligence they had received would be just north of La Paz. It was an area of about 20,000 acres scattered all along the edge of some mountainous terrain. Once again this patch appeared to be unattended at the moment of their assessment. From their map this appeared to be the Yungas area, which as near as they could tell was the second largest area of coca in the State of Bolivia. It likewise was unattended except for one man who was stirring a mixture of leaves. They did have a conversation with the attendant and it was a friendly meeting. Joe told him that they were inspectors who were there to ascertain that proper procedures were being followed.

When they had finished inspecting the area Joe asked if the keeper had ever heard of the Route 36 Club in La Paz. He said, "Oh yes, they have very good cocaine at that bar, not too far from this location. In fact, you can pay $10 and you get a drink of your choice and 1 mg of cocaine.

With that Joe and Cody decided they had what information they needed. They bade the nice gentleman good day and made their way back to the copter and they were off again assessing the surrounding areas. They knew that the amount of cocaine produced in each of these countries would vary from year to year, but they thought that this year Bolivia was in the process of producing between 50 to 60 thousand acres of coca plants and much of it was going to Europe and Asia rather than the U.S.

They camped in a secluded area not too far from La Paz for the night. They had predicted, by the intelligence briefing, that Peru or Colombia would have even more cocaine than Bolivia. But where was it going and how was it getting there? They were curious as to what they might learn if they were able to make it to the famous club called Route 36 in La Paz. Surely they could find out more about the shipping and handling of the cocaine if they could talk to more locals.

They made sure they landed and parked the copter in a location that was secluded but within walking distance of the edge of the city. They went on foot until they were able to flag down a cabbie. When they got in the car they asked that he take them to Route 36. He answered in Spanish, "I will if I can find it." He said that it moved around a lot so he might need to find another cabbie if it was not at the last location that he was familiar with. He took them to one location and sure enough it had moved. He then stopped another cabbie and found the new location. Within 5 minutes they were there. They tipped him and bade him farewell.

Once inside the club they found groups of people, including some Gringos mixed in, and this place was obviously a temporary address. They sat on a couple of stools at a table close to the bar where people were crowded around. The waiter said, "Drink of your choice and 1 mg of cocaine and that will be $10 American.

Both Joe and Cody consumed their cocktails leaving the cocaine on the table. They were carefully watching those around them and listening to all the casual conversation. Finally they overheard two men standing next to them discussing the cocaine they had just shipped and one of them asked, "How did you send it?" The other man responded that his shipment went to the U.S., but that it had to be sent by submarine because the U.S. Coast Guard now had fast boats that were too fast and could overtake their boats. So in order to get around that, Pablo Escobar and a few others were getting by the U.S. Coast Guard by sending the drugs by submarine. They commented that the U.S had successfully cut off the air and sea routes, but the subs were getting through because neither radar nor sonar could pick up the sub's signal. The one man went on to say that one of these subs could carry enough payload to be worth 200-400 million in street value. The first man went on to ask where the subs were being built and the other man responded that they were building them right in the jungle swamp areas from where they were launched. Some of them are being built pretty much on site in the marshy lowlands near the sea, both on the Pacific side and the Atlantic side.

He went on to say that the subs came in different sizes depending on how large the haul was to be and even if they lost a sub it only cost about 2 million to build another and depending on its size 2 million was peanuts compared to what one shipment of cocaine would make. The first man asked about the crew; to which the other man responded that there were crews of two to four depending on the size of the sub.

The one telling the story then said, "Looks like we have finally come up with the solution to the U.S. Coast Guard problem. We were getting along quite well going through Mexico until the Mexicans decided to take a major portion of the pie; then we had to come up with a way to bypass them." He then indicated that he was a close associate of Pablo Escobar, who was by now both widely respected and hated throughout the drug industry depending on one's perspective. He was already a hated and wanted criminal, or a modern day Robin Hood, depending on which side you were on. But he was also a folk hero because he gave much of his money to the poor.

The first man said to the other, "Then how are these subs powered?" To which the other man responded that they were being towed by fishing boats with long tow cables that allowed them to travel just a few inches below the water's surface so that it appears that the fishing boat is just trolling for fish. And if or when this method is discovered, they were also working on a diesel powered engine, super quiet that could be used by the sub to generate its own power.

Joe and Cody quietly left the club and they were both devastated by what they just heard. They tracked down a cab to take them back to the outskirts of the city where they had a short walk of a couple of miles to get back to their helicopter. By now it was almost midnight. Cody said to Joe before going to sleep, "Looks like we've already found out more than we had imagined." They crawled into their sleeping bags and slept until it was almost daylight.

Now they were ready to take a look at Peru to see how it fit into this puzzle. They took off and on the way to higher altitude they landed at one of the secret fuel facilities to fuel the copter; and while they were there they took a look at the mountainous country they were about to enter. They were awestruck by what they saw even though they had been thoroughly briefed on what to expect. Just the mere fact that the Andes Mountain range extended some 5500 miles from Peru to the end of Chile was in itself a marvel.

They also knew from their study of the area that the Apurimac River began in the Arequipa Province in the Southwestern mountain ranges of Peru, then gradually works its way around to a northeasterly heading and runs 528 miles, where it finally descends to an altitude of 860 feet above sea level, and in the process it picks up numerous other smaller streams as it works its way back eastward. The Apurimac River is formed in the beginning by melting glaciers, not the tallest of which is the Mismi Mountain which starts at 18,000 feet above sea level. This is the source or headwaters of the Amazon River. In its descent it is also joined by the Mantaro and Urbama Rivers. When the Apurimac is joined by the Ucayali River it then becomes the Ene River, and that eventually becomes the Tambo River and finally the Amazon. As these rivers join, one might say they form somewhat of a fertile delta region that grows anything well, but especially coca plants. Coca plants are "ubiquitous," literally meaning they are everywhere at the same time.

The people of this region had raised coca plants since the beginning of their time. They used it to relieve pain and even to treat hunger pangs. They were good, honest, hard working people who were mostly Catholic and worshiped accordingly. Peru was a province of Spain from about the 1500s until the Peruvian people fought for and were able to become an independent Republic in about 1821. To them, raising coca was a way of life. And there were at least 1,000 families who made their living by raising and selling coca. The sale of it brought them five times the amount of money that all their other crops did.

These people were poor by American standards and they could only afford to eat meat once weekly. Therefore they didn't understand why the U.S. was paying their government, the Peruvian government, to influence them not to grow coca. And if one could only stop and think, they had a valid point. The U.S. has poor people, true, but compared to what standard? Joe said to Cody, "If the poor people in the U.S. are so poor, then why are so many poor people from other countries trying to come to the U.S. to continue being poor?"

By daylight, Joe and Cody had eaten their rations and rolled up the sleeping bags. They already knew from what they had found in Bolivia that their reception in Peru would be positive as far as the native people would be concerned. They didn't know, however, what their reception would be like if they were greeted by other than the farmers. So they would err on the side of caution and try to put the copter down in a relatively remote spot and walk in. They would start in the area of the Ene River and work up or down the river from there. The sectional maps were showing the main areas they were interested in seeing. From the air they photographed the area and there were, by estimate, over 150,000 acres of coca at various stages of growth.

They landed the copter and walked in the direction of a field of coca. They met a man at the edge of the field and spoke to him in Spanish telling him they were interested in buying some coca. The man responded in Spanish that most of the farmers, including him, sold to the first one with the money. He said that was the way most farmers worked. But he also said that some cartels buy in large amounts, so it depended on the situation. He knew that Pablo Escobar had a large operation in the area. Cody asked if the coca making operations were here or did they, the customers, take the leaves to another location. He said that Pablo had numerous operations and that the coca was processed on site and then moved. He said he didn't know for sure how they moved it, but he thought some of it was moved by aircraft. Joe then asked if most of the growers were local mom and pop operations or were they owned by outside cartels. The man said it was a mix, but he thought it was about half and half. He said he could get more for his coca if he sold it himself, but that it was easier if he sold to Pablo, even though the profit would be a little less. And Pablo would send in his people to supervise the operation.

Cody said to the farmer, speaking in Spanish, "Are the fields of coca that Pablo Escobar owns guarded?" The man replied that he thought they were, that they had their process for making the cocaine which he had heard they would not share. Cody said, "Do you know anything about where the coca is transported or where it goes.?" The man answered that he had heard recent rumors about some of it being transported by submarine, but that he didn't know for sure. Though he did know that Pablo's operation was highly secretive. He also said that he had heard that some of Pablo's operation was near the coastline.

He went on to say that coca was their staple crop and he didn't understand why the Peruvian government, along with the U.S. government, was so intent on starving the 10,000 plus families that lived in this delta region. "We have been raising, using and selling our coca for thousands of years and all we ask is to be left alone. If people want to buy our coca, then come and buy it. If you no want it, then please stay away and leave us alone." He went on to say, "Now the Peruvian government comes around and wants to tell each farmer how much coca he can raise. Please just stay away and leave us alone."

Joe and Cody left and visited several other farms and the story was the same. They were greeted in a friendly manner and when they left the last farmer they were convinced that the problem was one of supply and demand. If there was a want or need for the coca, someone was going to raise it and supply it to the highest bidder.

Little known fact: the original Coca Cola drink had as part of its recipe, coca leaves, which contained a small amount of cocaine, along with some caffeine. That was in 1897 when the drink was first introduced. And it was advertised as a tonic. But in 1903 the recipe was changed to leave out the cocaine due to 'popular demand'.

Chapter 9
Dr. Joe's Medical Mission

THE LAST FARMER THEY visited with made the remark that his people were very sick. Joe asked what the problem was and the farmer said he wasn't sure what it was but that over the last 6 months they had already lost 3,000 people due to the disease. He said they were too poor to have a doctor in the community. The doctor in Joe sprang into action immediately. He asked the farmer what the disease looked like or what the symptoms were. The man, an Inca Indian, responded that the people who had the disease started out with a cough and fever and in about 2 weeks they began to have red spots. After another week or so the red spots became large blisters. After another week or two the blisters would burst and within 2 or 3 weeks the person would die. And when the blisters burst a milky fluid came out and they seemed to slough their skin and shortly after that, they would die. It seemed to be much worse in children and older people. And out of about 10,000 families in the area between 3,000 and 4,000 had died. Once one person in the home got it, the whole family got it.

At that point Dr. Joe told the farmer that he was a medical doctor and asked if he could see one of the sick people? The man asked Dr. Joe and Cody to follow him. Within a short walk they arrived at a house where Dr. Joe was taken to the bedside or a four-year-old girl. The first thing he noticed was that her face, arms and body were virtually covered with huge blisters that had a characteristic dimple in the center of the blister. No one had a flashlight, but he looked in her open mouth and saw the same lesions covering her mouth inside. She was obviously very ill and was not able to eat or drink. They had no thermometer but she was hot to the touch so he knew she had a high fever. Dr. Joe knew immediately that this was smallpox and that this little girl would be dead within a week or ten days if supportive care was not started.

Dr. Joe asked the farmer if there were many others in the community who looked like this. The farmer replied, "Yes, there are many others in the community like this." Out of desperation Dr. Joe asked where the local hospital was. To which the farmer replied, "We have none. We had a doctor, but he died a year ago and we can't get help from the government because they are too far away and it is so hard to get here. The mountain passages are unusable in winter because of the snow and in the summer there is rain and it is too muddy to travel." Dr. Joe then asked if they had a local church. To which the farmer replied, "Yes, it is about 2 miles down the river Ene." Dr Joe asked, "Can you take me there?"

When they arrived at the church the priest was most gracious and accommodating when Dr. Joe explained that there was an epidemic of smallpox in the community and that they must act quickly to isolate the sick from the healthy and they would need a place to put the sick. So the priest offered to use the church as a hospital where they could treat the sick. He would have the parish members move the pews out to make a hospital ward out of the church. Then Dr. Joe asked if the priest knew Pablo Escobar well enough that he might prevail upon him to help with their cause. The priest said there were members of his congregation who worked for Pablo and he would ask one of them. In fact, just as he made that statement one of them came through the door. The man whom the priest spoke to said that he could leave at that moment to find Pablo. Dr. Joe gave a list of hospital equipment they would need, including beds, lab equipment, plasma, IV fluids and antibiotics, to increase the survival rate. Joe knew there was a new mycin drug out that would kill some of the larger viruses.

Dr. Joe remembered from medical school that there were two types of smallpox viruses, one called the major and the other called the minor smallpox virus. The major was called Variola major and its counterpart was called Variola minor. The incubation period for either was 7 to 14 days. The major virus would go inside the cells of the body and cause swelling of the cells. Typical flu-like symptoms would occur, fever, nausea and vomiting, muscle and joint pain with headache and back pain. The major virus could invade the gastrointestinal track as well, in which case it could cause sloughing of the intestinal lining followed by hemorrhage and death.

This disease had been avoidable since the 1700s when a vaccination was discovered by Edward Jenner using cowpox. It should be mentioned that there are other pox viruses that are benign including chickenpox, and monkeypox, but they can be managed and are not malignant.

The only one Joe knew of around the area who had the money to right this situation was the drug lord Pablo Escobar. He was said to be a modern day Robin Hood who championed the cause of the poor and oppressed. It might be worth a try to reach out to him since Pablo was one of the principals involved in the Ene valley cocaine business.

Dr. Joe and Cody had been vaccinated for smallpox so there was little risk of their contracting the disease. The priest sent the messenger directly to Pablo to inform him that they had a doctor; but that they were desperately in need of the equipment and medical supplies to equip a hospital. Otherwise they would lose the entire community. Within three days many medical supplies arrived and Dr. Joe and his assistant, Cody, were busy with their humanitarian duties of treating the sick in their makeshift church hospital.

It took exactly three days for twenty-five hospital beds and all the equipment of a modern hospital to arrive. If anyone had ever doubted the sincerity of Pablo Escobar where help for the truly needy was concerned this answered that question. He was known for helping the poor who were in need.

The first patient Dr. Joe and Cody saw was the four-year-old girl who had a worst case of the disease. She was now covered with blisters which had already begun to burst and they were oozing a yellowish fluid which Dr. Joe thought was body proteins. They started with a battery of lab work, IV fluids, and antibiotics to cover the skin infection already obvious as they did appropriate cultures.

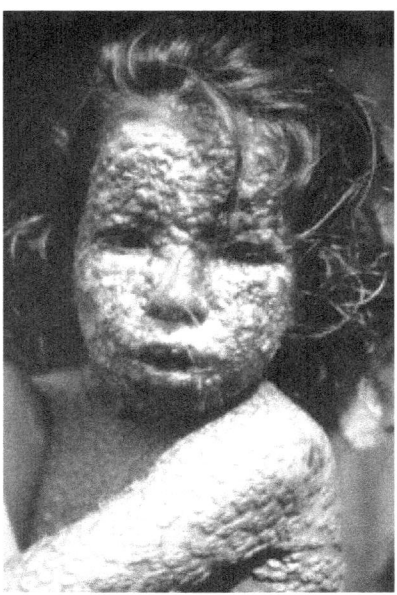

Providers 3265: CDC/James Hicks

BEFORE THEY COULD GET the first patient worked up they would have a second case roll through the door. This patient was an older case than the first one, a seven-year-old male. Most of the large blisters had burst and Dr. Joe could see that much of the epidermis had been shed from his body. Only the underlying dermis, the second layer, was left without a way to keep out infection. Numerous areas of the dermis had pustular drainage. But Dr. Joe had done a rotation on general surgery and knew how to skin graft.

There was a local native, an Inca Indian woman, who was also helping who knew a little about anesthesia as she had worked a bit with the previous doctor. Dr. Joe knew no one had anything to lose in this situation, so with some brief instruction they were able to put the boy under light general anesthesia. Joe did skin grafts from some of the areas that were not affected. The surgery and recovery were successful. They ran a battery of lab tests. They also asked all the native population to come for blood typing to offer blood to these needy patients. This little guy was still alive 3 days post-op. There was now a ray of hope that what they were doing was helping.

The very first day they filled all the hospital beds and needed more, but they were limited as to the caregivers they had. They tried to treat the sickest patients first, and as expected children and old people were the first to get hit with the disease and also the most likely to die.

The third patient Dr. Joe and Cody saw was an 84-year-old male. He was hemorrhaging from his bowels and there did appear to be tissue in his bowel movements. He had a hemoglobin of 7. Dr. Joe knew they needed type O negative blood and lots of it; anyone can receive type O negative blood. However all were invited to give blood. The 84-year-old was typed and matched for blood and found to be A positive. They were having many donors. Dr. Joe gave plasma in hopes of restoring some of the proteins that this patient was losing. He started the new mycin antibiotic in hopes of getting him some relief. Joe, Cody, the priest and the one lady who had some medical knowledge background took vital signs every 15 minutes on all the patients.

The church hospital was full before the first day had passed. They had 14 pediatric patients, 6 adult working age patients and 5 elderly patients. The 4-year-old girl that they had admitted the first day coded the next morning. Dr. Joe had done a chest x-ray on admission which revealed minimal perihilar congestion. She had been given IV fluids and antibiotics with vitamins since admission. Then she had gone into ventricular fibrillation. The paddles were used a number of times in an effort to convert her to normal rhythm, but to no avail. The priest did last rites and she was removed from the hospital.

Before they knew it, more were there for admission. The census stayed at 25. The elderly man who had been admitted with the bleeding intestinal problem was now in great in distress as he was still hemorrhaging even though he been given whole blood and platelets as well. A STAT EKG was done which revealed ventricular tachycardia. Dr. Joe knew they had to get this converted fast or they would be a dollar late so to speak. He did do a cardioversion on him successfully, so for now at least things were okay with this elderly patient. Dr. Joe really didn't see how he could survive and at that very moment the patient straight lined on the EKG. Dr. Joe's better judgement prevailed and he called the priest. He knew he would lose at least 30% of these patients even with the best effort to save them. And there were more waiting outside the doors of the church.

This virus, the Variola major dates back about as far as history goes. Even as late as the 18th Century it took more than 400,000 lives in Europe. But there was even a greater threat to mankind that goes back to the 15th century and earlier. It was called at the time the Great Pox.

Joe and Cody continued this effort for 2 months before a medical team finally arrived from Lima, Peru. At that point they relinquished their caregiver duties to the incoming medical team.

Chapter 10
Back to the DEA Mission and Subs

THEY NOW WENT BACK to their copter and plotted their next move. By now Cody and Joe had found that there were 300,000 acres plus or minus being grown in the three countries, Columbia, Bolivia and Peru depending on which state was under the most scrutiny by the world order at the moment. As they saw it, their next move should be to find out as much as possible about whether the movement by submarine was a reality or just a lot of talk.

They spent most of the day going over the maps of the Colombian coastline in an effort to find where the likely area or areas would be to launch a submarine, if there even was such a thing. They then visited another of their secret fueling locations and topped off the fuel tank. They pretty well knew that to build the sub within the city and then move it to the coast would not be very smart or very secret. They had in their packet of maps some maps that were 1:100,000 in scale of the coastal areas of Colombia. They knew that the area would need to have a good jungle cover so that the area would have a natural camouflage but the water needed to be deep enough to float the sub out of there once it was built and stocked. After looking at all the options they finally decided that they would need to fly the copter near the areas of interest and walk in.

They had in their possession a set of inflatable pontoons for the chopper should they ever need them. The only problem was that they were very limited as far as airspeed was concerned with the inflatables. This being the case, they needed to get as close as they could before using them because they would collapse at any airspeed of more than 25 miles per hour, making it a perfect target for ground fire. If they had known in advance that they would need pontoons, they could have had permanent pontoons put on the aircraft before they left Panama. So much for coulda, woulda, shoulda, right? They were stuck with having to put on the disposables or land the copter on hard ground and walk in on foot, which made the operation much more hazardous. Rule #1, don't run off without your copter or you may not get back to it or someone might just steal it; or worse yet, they might shoot you when you return. Now as one can clearly see, none of these are good options.

If they used the disposable pontoons, it would be necessary for them not put them on until they knew they were near the area they needed to inspect. And in order to deploy them Cody would need to hold the copter in a hover just a few feet off the ground while Joe deployed them. Once they were deployed, Joe could climb back inside the copter and they could literally slow fly the coastline until they saw the area they were looking for and then put the copter down on the water a safe distance away and wade into the area in question.

The longer they looked at the maps the more they began to realize that the only sensible way to do this part of the mission might be to slow fly the jungle in grid fashion while shooting a mosaic picture run with the camera. That way there was a good chance of seeing the right place or places on film review even if they made no visual contact at the time they flew over it. But that was also a very good way to alert the enemy of their presence. A large number of these finger waterways make their way inland from the shores of Ecuador and also Colombia. Joe and Cody knew they didn't want to return home without the goods they sought. They were both seasoned veterans and felt that this was the most important mission in which they had ever participated. So they began to fly the swampy jungle in grid fashion.

They had decided to begin their work near the Ecuadorian border. Once they arrived at the border, they began slow flying the waterways that ran back into the jungle. Some of them were miles long. They were then hit with the realization that building and hiding a sub in this area would not be difficult at all.

You wouldn't believe this unless you saw it with your very own eyes, but look what Joe and Cody found sitting right on the Ecuadorian-Colombian border. And they got the pictures to prove it.

DEA Press Release: photographer Christoph Morlinghaus

JOE AND CODY DECIDED to land and gather more information about this very obvious Narc Sub, since it appeared that there was no one around the area at the time. Fortunately they were able to find a small opening in the canopy of the jungle about 100 yards away from the site so Cody, being the expert copter pilot that he was, put it down right on the spot.

They knew the risk was extreme; but they also knew that their mission was of utmost importance to the war on drugs. They walked into the site at a rapid pace. Once they arrived at the sub, Cody stood guard while Joe went inside it to see what, if any, navigation equipment was on board, and to photograph the inside. Joe was astonished at the level of sophistication. They had a celestial navigation system that could be used if they were not under eminent attack and they also had a satellite navigation system. It had TACAN and VOR equipment so that they could rendezvous with their counterparts without making landfall. This made navigation easy. They could go direct or they could intersect with any radial of the U.S. navigation facilities they decided to use and meet their pick-up guys at any predetermined point. This was not to mention that the pick-up point could be changed on a moment's notice if they were in contact with the pick-up guys. They even had a code for communication. They had virtually thought of everything. Joe stuck the written code in his pocket just in time to hear Cody yell, "COME ON, LETS GET OUT OF HERE !!!" It was an hour past the noon hour and Joe and Cody knew the crew had come back from their lunch break. Joe scampered out of the sub and they ran as fast as possible towards the copter. The bullets were flying all around them but they managed to get back inside the copter where the bullet proof windshield saved them from being hit. Cody quickly started the engine, which was already under fire, but it had bullet proofing. It started and Cody lifted off the ground quickly. But the blades were hit by some of the bullets so the copter was vibrating due to the chunks taken from the bullet resistant blades.

Cody was able to get the craft flying anyway and he headed directly to the coast as soon as they were airborne. The hail of bullets continued as Cody flew the vibrating craft toward the coastline, which was only a short distance away. They immediately picked the heading towards Panama and began to Squawk Emergency on the IFF, which they knew would alert the good guys of the U.S. Coast Guard. They knew that this would be a short flight because they knew for sure the vibration of the blades would lead to engine failure and ditching at sea more likely sooner than later.

With this in mind, they both donned their life vests and Joe put all their intelligence film and evidence in a safe floating raft in case of their own demise. The aircraft continued to vibrate such that they could not see the engine gauges, so they knew ditching into the water could come at any moment. The question was whether they could get far enough out that the U.S. Coast Guard could get to them before the Narco guys did.

They had made it out to sea about 50 miles when the engine began to seize. With this sobering reality in mind, Cody was flying the aircraft very close to the water so at the precise moment the engine seized, he could just drop it into the water. Joe and Cody could see through the rear view mirror that the Narco guys were in hot pursuit in a speed boat. Just as the engine was beginning to seize, Cody stopped the copter and put it in the water, and as they were ditching they grabbed their AR15s and jumped, inflating their rafts as they hit the water. They began firing on the approaching Narco guys. Joe and Cody never said it to each other before but they both knew they would never be taken alive. Suddenly the attacking Narco guys made an immediate 180 degree turn and headed back the other way.

In all the excitement of defending themselves Joe and Cody had failed to see the U.S. Coast Guard speed boat coming from the other direction. Once Joe and Cody were safely aboard all Joe could say was, **_"It's sure good to see you guys!"_**

Chapter 11
Home to Lisa & Back to ER Practice

AFTER BEING PICKED up by the US Coast Guard, Joe and Cody were taken back to Panama. They were debriefed by the DEA in the DEA hanger briefing room. And the DEA was both surprised and pleased by what they had found. They were particularly surprised to find that the drugs were being delivered by submarine. This filled in a lot of blanks as to how these deadly drugs were getting into the United States. They had the pictures to prove how it was being done. Now the U.S. government would be able to take their case directly the governments involved and get a solution to the problem. And Cody and Dr. Joe would be able to return home with the pleasure of knowing that they had made another great contribution to their country.

Cody was a rancher in real life so he would return to Montana near Great Falls and back to his ranch and Joe could now return to his Emergency Room medical practice and to his family. When Dr. Joe stepped of the airplane at the Meridian Airport, Lisa and the kids were there to meet him and it was quite a home coming. The four kids were now 17, 13, 12 and 11. And the two older kids were both in college now pursuing their degrees in Nursing and Dentistry. They all went home and had a great celebration that evening. Lisa had a huge turkey dinner prepared with some great white wine to go with it. After a short nap, Joe told them as much as he could about his and Cody's mission without getting into anything classified. Then Joe took a week off before return-ing to his work as an ER physician.

BACK TO ER PRACTICE IN FT. PAYNE, AL

After a relaxing week, Dr. Joe returned to his Emergency Room work at the Ft. Payne, AL hospital. The staff was all glad to see his safe return and he was glad to be back. Ft. Payne stands out because it is situated in the northwest corner of the State of Alabama and is the principal hospital for an area called Sand Mountain. Joe was the Emergency Room Director there before he left on his secret mission to South America. He told them as much as he could about his absence and his secret mission. Everyone seemed to realize the nature and secrecy of the mission and did not insist on his elaborating it.

Things sometimes seem to work out the way they should and sometimes they work out the way they shouldn't. Joe actually would finally come to the conclusion that, in fact, things always work out the way they should, just depends on how you look at it. And some months later, Dr. Joe had been doing ER medicine long enough that he finally realized that he wasn't bullet proof after all. He was now getting tired of looking at that ER door and never knowing what was coming through there next. He was a good doc and could take care of anyone who was sick, but his body was showing the signs of wear. He knew that he could not keep up the torrid pace that he had set for himself over the years; something had to give. He was overweight and felt that he was losing the battle with age, or at least it seemed so to him. He and Lisa got along as well as they always had but he wanted to feel better and look better.

The older two children had moved to Mississippi so they could be closer to their Dad and also to complete their higher educations. The eldest girl, Lou, had finished her nursing school education at the University of Southern Mississippi in Hattiesburg, had married, and was a nurse practitioner in south Florida. The eldest son, Thomas, had finished his dental school degree at the University of Mississippi Dental School and opened his general dentistry practice in Brandon, MS near Jackson. Both were doing well and soon Thomas would have a new addition to his family, a son. Four years later they would have a second addition to their family, another son.

Lisa's daughter, Lee Ann, was now 17 and graduating from high school. She had decided to follow in her mother's footsteps and pursue a law degree at Ole Miss.

Meanwhile, the younger three children Cindy, Lindy, and Donald were growing up fast. Since Joe had been absent for so long on his secret missions, time seemed to slip away even faster. All three were in the private school system. Joe and Lisa had opted to send them to private school because they wanted them to be educated, not indoctrinated. And they were all doing well.

Both of the girls took dancing from the time they were just toddlers all the way through high school and were active as cheerleaders. And remarkably, both of them were homecoming queens a year apart. You just can't imagine how proud Dr. Joe was to be able to escort the homecoming queen out onto the football field at halftime two years in a row. In her senior year of high school, Cindy played the lead in the Nutcracker Suite Ballet and Lindy danced in the show as well. Joe would like to think they got their good looks from him but that's neither here nor there. Joe thought the song went something like this, "They have their mama's good looks and their daddy's wallet."

Author photo

ALSO, IT SHOULD BE mentioned that Donald, the youngest of Joe's five children, achieved his Eagle Boy Scout rank while he was still in his 13th year. This is a feat seldom reached by a young boy. Lisa was so proud of all of them that she could hardly hold back the tears of joy. There was no doubt about it, they were growing up way too fast.

But Joe felt fat and out of shape and he didn't like feeling that way. So he decided he would start a walking program to try getting back into good physical condition. He started right out walking 5 miles a day and immediately noticed that he felt better with the exercise program. Soon he began to time his walks, since he walked the same route each day. He was also heavier than he remembered being in his lifetime so he began to check his weight daily, weighing at the same time each morning when he first got out of bed. Within just a few days he was feeling better and also he began to lose some of that 205 lbs. he'd been carrying. He had been doing this walking routine for about 2 weeks when one day he broke into a trot, but this didn't last long before he had to walk again.

This went on over a period of a few weeks until he was slow running the entire course. Joe continued increasing the pace and distance until within a month he was running the whole 5 mile course. He gradually picked up the pace and the distance and the pounds came rolling off. Then he got serious about this and began to run longer and faster. For this program, he needed a special watch so he could time his distance and speed. He became aware that there were other people doing the same thing he was doing and soon he met some of these people. Each had different goals but all were in it to feel good and look better.

It was along about this time that he discovered that there were races around the local area for those who wanted to compete for the sport of it. Joe found that there was a local 5K race coming up soon in the Meridian area and he figured, 'Oh what the heck, I might as well try it'. Joe ran his first 5K race 2 months after he had began walking and would you believe he won his age group. No big deal, but it was good clean fun.

Azalea Trail Run, March 23, 1995 Marathon Foto

JOE SOON FOUND THAT these people who jogged for health also hung around together as friends. Joe discovered that the more he ran, the more friends he made who were runners. The runners all shared a common goal of getting their bodies in better shape and keeping them that way. Within the next few weeks Joe had run in two 10K races and this took him over to the Jackson area where he made more friends and all the time he was getting faster.

Finally he was told that there was a big Marathon coming up in Huntsville, Alabama. He made up his mind to try it. He told Lisa and she was very excited over the prospect, but she said, "Isn't it a bit early to try one of those?" Joe said, "Maybe, but I want to try it anyway." Joe hit the running books and the training calendar. He already had his weight down to 160 lbs. from 205 lbs. and by his computations if he could run at least one 20 miler in practice 2 weeks before the big race, he might just be able to do it. According to his sources he needed to work on speed as well but he would need to run the 20 miler 2 weeks before and get plenty of rest in the last week of practice. Lisa was so sweet and understanding of this compulsive warrior.

Lisa made the family hotel reservations in Huntsville for the great race. Joe had talked to some of his running buddies about the marathon. And they were all resolute about saying that you will never have a greater physical challenge in your life than running in it. The marathon has no friend. Everyone suffers and everyone hits the wall at 20 miles. When you get to 20 miles it becomes a question of how bad do you really want this because by then the marathon has taken its toll on you. Sheer determination not to let that race beat you into the ground is what it takes to do that last 10K.

So Lisa and the three youngest kids arrived in Huntsville the late evening before the big race and were greeted with a big spaghetti dinner which was thrown for all the racers. This was only 4 months after the first time Joe had put his shoes on to walk. The morning of the great race Joe felt well and was ready to give it his best shot. He started at about the middle of the pack. He noticed there were all kinds of people and athletes starting this race, from short to tall, fat to slim, and some really great young runners. Joe was 49-years-old and wanted to do a respectable job on this race; but he wasn't trying to set any kind of a land speed record so he just fell into a pace that he thought he could sustain for the long haul. He did this for the first 5 miles and things were going well enough that he picked up the pace a little. Finally by the 10 mile marker the nonserious group was beginning to drop out of the race. And by 15 miles this race was beginning to wear on everyone. At that point it had become serious business. Joe was holding up very well, but for the first time he was beginning to feel tired. Many runners were dropping out of the race now and it had lost its luster of just a fun jog. But then the 18 mile mark went by and Joe was beginning to think that there really wasn't much to this thing. All at once things changed drastically at about 19 and a half miles. Suddenly there was pain in areas that Joe couldn't imagine and he was getting short of breath too. When he passed the 20 mile marker he was beginning to think that God was punishing him for all his sins. And then he realized that there was a real possibility that he might not finish this race after all. Finally at 22 miles Joe's pace had slowed to almost a standstill and it was all he could do to keep putting one foot in front of the other. Joe had thought at 16 miles that he would finish in under 3 hours. But it was quite amazing how quickly that lofty goal fell by the wayside as he struggled to stay in the race after 20 miles. Everyone, every racer, hits what is called "the wall" at 20 miles. From Joe's knowledge of anatomy and physiology, he believed that 20 miles was about the design limit of the human body. After struggling from mile 22 to mile 26 Joe could finally see the finish at a distance with only about a half mile to go and it was all he could do to make the finish line in 3 hours and 52 minutes. For all that hard work he did have his picture taken as he crossed the finish line.

Author photo

LISA AND THE KIDS WERE there at the finish line cheering him on. Joe was so beaten that he laid flat on his back for about 5 minutes before he could get back onto his feet.

Joe would be the first to tell you that not everyone is capable of doing a marathon; but no matter how good an athlete you are, the marathon is the biggest athletic challenge you will ever face.

The next marathon Dr. Joe ran was in New Orleans in January. He trained for the race and had his schedule made up to attend. He and Lisa left the kids with friends for the weekend. The race was a Sunday morning event. They had flown down in the Bonanza the night before and parked it at the New Orleans Airport and flagged down taxi to get to the Sheraton Hotel which was near the end of Bourbon Street. Once checked into the hotel it was 9 pm and time to make it on down to Bourbon Street to have some of that fine New Orleans food and listen to some of that fine Dixieland Jazz music. Lisa was overcome by all the strange looking people.

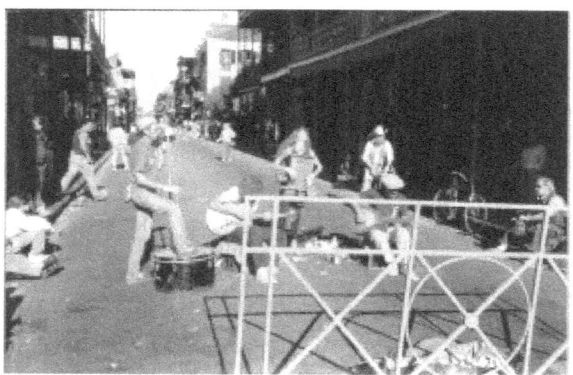

Author photo

THEY DANCED A FEW TIMES and turned in early because the racers briefing would be at 8:00 in the morning. When they got to the race area there was already a large crowd waiting. They started on standard Louisiana time, a half hour late. It was a cool morning though not too cool for shorts. There were about 1000 racers and once they were briefed, or shortly thereafter, the race began. The pace was not too fast so Joe took a position about a third of the way to the rear and as the crowd cleared out he gradually move toward the front. This was mostly a new or different group of runners of whom he recognized none. By now Joe was a lot more marathon savvy than he had been in the earlier races. He was in good physical condition and had weighed in the day before at 158 lbs. He felt good. As he went along he gradually picked up the pace and at thirteen miles he thought he was on schedule to run about a 3:30 minute marathon. At 20 miles, like everyone else, he was in pain, but barring no unforeseen problems he should do a 3:30 marathon. He was wasted at 20 miles but his time was better than on previous races and he was on schedule to set a new personal best. This time he crossed the finish at 3 hours and 32 minutes and this was a new personal best. The weather had been ideal and he did win his age group that day. He was now in the 50-54 age group.

Every athlete who is a marathoner has a few races that stand out in his or her mind as being special. Before you know the particulars of the race though, you need to know a little about the events leading up to the race. Dr. Joe had a good friend who was at the time the dentist for the same Air Guard unit in which Joe was the flight surgeon. Dr. Joe may not have gotten into Marathons if it had not been for Dr. Joe Robinson, his dentist friend. They did several marathons together and Dr. Robinson always won the race between the two of them, not by much but enough to finish ahead of Dr. Joe. So there was a friendly rivalry.

There was a big marathon race coming up which Dr. Joe had never run before but his dental friend had run in it. It was called the Scottish Marathon. It began on the University of Asheville grounds, near the Smokey Mountains, and wound back towards Cherokee, North Carolina and then the last half of the race would wind its way up through the Smokey Mountains, going uphill all the way until the finish on top of one of the mountain peaks.

When it was time for the race to begin that Saturday morning, Joe and his dentist friend got off with the other 1000 runners headed across the first half. Joe knew what to expect because his friend had briefed him ahead of time. It was a nice morning and off they went, all 1000 of them. The first part or half of the race was just ho-hum, up and down a number of small peaks and also a lot of level ground. Everyone seemed to be going along okay. There were a lot of runners who had done this race before and everyone sort of settled into their own race at their own pace. Joe had left his friend behind a long while ago and was moving on with the race at his own pace. It's really hard to tell you how a race like this started as something totally innocuous and in the end will just eat your heart out as it slowly chews you and spits you out in the last 6 miles. Joe was beating his good friend to the finish but then came miles 25 and 26 which were straight up hill. Dr. Joe's pace had slowed to a snail's pace by now. He was really struggling to stay in the race. At 1/2 mile from the finish Joe's friend caught up and barely eased by him 100 feet before the finish and as his friend got alongside him, his friend said, "I thought I would never catch you." His friend finished 20 feet ahead of Joe.

But they both enjoyed hearing the Scottish bagpipes playing, complete with the bagpipers wearing their traditional short plaid kilts. It was a great celebration and a great party. Joe had never before or since run a marathon that went straight up the side of a mountain to the finish. In spite of losing the race to his good friend by 20 feet both Dr. Joe and his friend had a great day.

Dr. Joe had become interested in swimming and cycling as well. After he had done 12 marathons he was wanting to mix running, cycling and swimming. So, he did a few biathlons where there would be a 10K race and then maybe a 20 or 30 mile bike race. Then he decided to try his hand at doing a triathlon where there was a half mile swim, then a 25 or 30 mile bike segment and then a foot race to finish. The sense of all this is that some people are better at certain sports than others. It doesn't make anyone look bad to be better at one sport than the other. Many experts think that the triathlete is the best of all because he or she can do all three sports well when considered as a mix.

So Dr. Joe began swimming and to his surprise he found that he was an excellent swimmer for any age group. He was much faster at swimming than his age group. And he could bike or cycle at about the 85th percentile level in his age group. He was about a 75th percentile level in running, so he was always competitive in his age group, and he signed up for his first triathlon.

Joe's 1st triathlon was the Neshoba County Triathlon. It started near Louisville with a 1/4 mile swim followed by a 30 mile bike ride and finally ending in a 5 mile run, which finished at the Neshoba county fairgrounds. The swim was an out and back type swim and there were about 500 contestants. There were fifteen in Joe's age group. Joe got a good start. Swimming was his best sport and he was in the lead group coming out of the water at the end of the swim. He quickly put on his biking shoes and was on the bike headed for the final leg of the race which would be the run. Joe was a good cyclist for his age group and he rode with the lead group through the bike part of the race. Every one ran at his or her own pace, however Joe finished the 30 mile bike portion still in good position. At the end of the bike portion it was necessary to park the bike at a predetermined area, put on his running shoes and run the last 5 miles on foot. Joe was quick to get his shoes on and step into the 5 mile run to the finish. He knew there a couple of guys who would be challenging him in the run and he knew that he was ahead of them by at least a minute when he got off the bike. He ran the first 3 miles of the run like his life depended on it so as not to give either of them time to catch him. Finally for the last 2 miles he slowed just a bit to a pace he knew he could sustain. No one challenged. He won his division.

Author photos

THE FINISH LINE WAS in front of the grand stand at the fair-grounds and there was a gala celebration already starting. It was high noon on Saturday. This was part of an annual celebration held yearly at the Neshoba county Fairgrounds.

Joe went on to run a number of triathlons, the longest of which was a 1/2 Ironman which turned out to be a 1 mile swim, 60 miles one the bike and a 10 mile run. After that one Joe decided that a trip to Hawaii for the real Ironman would require much more time and training than he was able to give. One of the first things a triathlete becomes aware of is that there is the Ironman Triathlon. The Ironman Triathlon is a 2.4 mile swim, then a 112 mile bike race and finishes with a marathon, 26.2 mile, foot race. This race is considered the ultimate triathlon. And only athletes who are the very best in all three sports compete.

Dr. Joe thought the Ironman was a great idea but he didn't think he would ever be able to devote the time it took to prepare and do that race. So it would have to be one of those things you just didn't get done. He was far too busy with family and other activities. Besides his younger children were entering college now and those obligations were first and foremost on his mind at the moment.

It was time to visit with his daughter in Florida, who was now a nurse practitioner. She and her husband had a sail boat and Dr. Joe and Lisa were anxious to go sailing with them. They left the three younger kids to the supervision of the grandparents and headed for Florida. Upon reaching Ft. Lauderdale where the kids lived, they were welcomed with all smiles and a packed agenda. They visited for a long weekend and had some really great food while they were there. The next day after they arrived they packed up for a long sailing journey.

Author photo

THEY FOUND A DOCKING place about 10 miles south of Miami where they docked at about 5 in the afternoon and started up the grill and cooked some burgers and wieners. The weather was just the right temperature and while the grandkids were swimming around the boat they all had a great time. Too soon it was time to head back to the home boat dock. They had a wonderful day and a great visit. They also visited the Everglades while they were there. This was certainly a wonderful place to visit but not to stay for long unless you had a cure for the mosquitoes. They visited around several areas and found that gators of all sizes and descriptions were found there. The gators were afraid of people and kept their distance and that was a good thing. There were 2 grandchildren there, both girls and they were such fun to get to know.

After a four day visit Joe and Lisa packed up and headed back home. They needed to get back to Meridian to check on their other three children. After two days on the road they were back in Meridian. The oldest two of the younger three were now in college and the youngest, Donald, was now a senior in high school. And Joe had retired from the Air Guard and was now headed back to the University in Jackson to pursue training in psychiatry.

During this time, Joe was still concerned about the toll that ER work was taking on him and his family. He remembered an old classmate with whom he had gone to medical school and interned. He was in psychiatry in Jackson and he thought he would give him a call. He did so and the old friend was glad to hear from Joe and said that he was on good and close terms with the doctor in charge of the residency program. A few phone calls and Dr. Joe was interviewing for the Psychiatry Residency Program. Dr. Joe knew that he still had kids in school though and he would still need to work nights and weekends in the ER to support his family. Lisa was working as well but it took a lot of money to support the needs of the 3 remaining children in school.

It was about this time that an old friend of Dr. Joe's called and asked if Joe would be interested in working two weekends a month at a small hospital just about 50 miles south of Montgomery, Alabama. Joe told him that he was back in residency training and would not be interested if it was too busy. He needed time to rest and study psychiatry. His friend said that it would be the right place for that.

Joe started his residency July 1st, 1987, the year after he retired from the Air Guard. During his residency program, he worked nights and weekends in the Emergency Rooms in Alabama and the surrounding area. That was the only way Joe could go back into residency based on their financial needs. However the ERs were not nearly as busy as they would become later. Thus he had plenty of time and nothing to do but study psychiatry during much of his time in the ER. If that sounds too good to be true, it's not, because ER medicine only paid about 22 to 25 dollars per hour in those days. So look at the numbers. You go to work at 6:00 pm on Friday and work until 6:00 am Monday and you find that it's a living, but you're not getting rich. And to keep his sanity and stay married to Lisa he had to be with the family one weekend a month. Sound busy? You bet he was!

Dr. Joe's old friend from the ER in Ft. Payne called about this time and asked him if he would consider working the ER two or three weekends a month, alternating with him at the hospital at Laverne, AL. He said it was not all that busy and it would probably tie in real well with his residency schedule. And he would able leave his ER job on Monday morning at 6:00 am and drive home in time to change clothes and go to work at the University. About this time Dr. Joe also began working on Thursday nights at another small town hospital in Waynesboro, MS and he would work there for years to come. Incidentally, the chair of psychiatry was a great psychiatrist and a fine gentleman, Dr. Edger Draper. Joe had never known a nicer man. Dr. Joe by now was tired of doing the heavy lifting of fairly busy ERs anyway, so he said yes to his friend, Stuart, at Laverne, AL.

As you may recall, a few years back Joe had also realized that he needed to take better care of his body, so over the past few years he had run 12 marathons and done numerous triathlons, along with a string of 5 and 10 k races. Was he able to do all this and keep up a busy work schedule, you bet. He probably wouldn't appreciate how busy he was in those days until his later years. When he first started he was 72 inches tall and weighed 205 pounds. Over the first 3 months he exercised he lost 45 pounds and was down to 160 pounds. And, he had weighed in after a marathon at as little as 148 pounds. He felt better than he ever had in his life. He would continue to jog for exercise but had to greatly limit the racing due to time constraints of his work schedule. There were times when there were no patients to see in the ER and Joe would go out and jog around the hospital within sight and calling distance of the ER. He was always where the ER nurse could summon him within 5 seconds. And there were times when he would change into his jogging shorts and run immediately after the relieving doctor arrived. Where there is a need, you find a way. Busy? Yes.

Chapter 11
PSYCHIATRY RESIDENCY

AT THE TIME DR. JOE returned to the University for psychiatry residency the feminist movement in the universities was just hitting full throttle and overdrive at the same time. He had never seen such surly women in his life. Every minute he was thinking, "What did I do to piss her off? I just can't believe what I'm seeing. What's with all this constant anger from women in the University system?" As he began to look into the situation, he found that the ring leaders in this new white man hating cult were Ruth Bader Ginsburg and Hillary Rodham Clinton. (Bill Clinton on advice of Janet Reno, his Attorney General, had appointed Ginsburg to the Supreme Court and the country became worse off today because of it. And today it looks as though she may outlive everyone. Two years later, to make matters worse, just look at what Obama appointed, two more just like her.)

Anyway, Dr. Joe remembered that there were 2 female residents appointed with him and one Indian male resident. Joe did have a short visit with one of the two female residents during their first week of residency and that one was a very nice person; but unfortunately she must have been quite depressed, because a week later she committed suicide by shooting herself. The other female resident let herself be known by telling Dr. Joe not to write any orders on her patients but to have the nurse call her if any orders were needed in her absence. The third resident, who was a male Indian type, was friendly and he and Dr. Joe got along very well.

Also the dress code had changed at the University since Joe was last there. It had changed from a dress shirt and tie culture to just anything you wanted to wear, including jeans and sandals or whatever. It all looked pretty sloppy to Joe but it wasn't his call to make as to what appearing to be professional was supposed to look like. "It's a pretty sorry scene though when you can't tell the patient from the doctor," he thought.

Dr. Joe's first rotation was at the Veteran's Administration Hospital Psychiatry Ward on the hill across from the University Hospital. Dr. Joe knew he was in the right place when he unlocked the door to the ward and walked in and there stood a man in the hallway masturbating. Dr. Joe advised him to step into the bathroom and went on with his rounds. The VA was certainly an interesting place to work. There were many patients who were treated for PTSD (post traumatic stress disorder). After taking a long look at the history of these patients, Dr. Joe found that most of the patients had some kind of nervous disorder before they went into the military, not all of them, but the vast majority. There certainly were some who were legitimate, but there were many alcoholics and drug addicts among them. Presenting themselves as PTSD made it next to impossible for the doctor to make an accurate call. There were many others who made the trip into combat and back and kept their sanity. So how do you explain the difference? And, of course, they talk among themselves and seemed at times to copy the symptoms of other patients.

Dr. Joe would later find, in child psychiatry, some of the mothers would have the textbook memorized regarding the symptoms of ADHD (attention deficit hyperactivity disorder) too. This made it difficult for the doctor when he is sitting right there with the patient and did not see the symptoms that the mother said she was seeing. He learned that about half of the ADHD patients overcame their disease by the time they were adults.

At the end of his 2nd year in residency, there was a vacancy in the child and adolescent psychiatry program and Joe thought it a great opportunity to super specialize in Children and Adolescent Psychiatry. Over the next two years he would work very closely with his mentor and supervisor Dr. Wood Hiatt. Dr. Hiatt was a fountain of knowledge and Joe took full advantage of it.

Dr. Joe was asked by the department to do a grand rounds study of Fetal Alcohol Syndrome (FAS). He spent 2 months doing all the research. What he found was that most of the organ systems of the fetus develop between the 4th and 12th week of pregnancy. Some women are vulnerable to this syndrome which causes wide and varied birth defects. His research showed in the 1st trimester of pregnancy that alcohol caused facial abnormalities and decreased growth rate of the baby in utero. He also would find that in the 2nd trimester of pregnancy, alcohol caused lowered IQ, further growth rate retardation, and deficits in math, reading and spelling skills. And in the 3rd trimester a further decrease in birth weight and potential height.

The bad part about all this was that there was no way to quantify the amount of alcohol consumed to the severity of the birth defects. Meaning that some women are more sensitive to alcohol than others. His ultimate determination was that no woman should drink any alcohol if she is or may become pregnant.

Now we should mention here a bit about how the State of Mississippi runs its mental health care program. First of all it is run by the Mississippi Psychological Association, not to be confused with the Mississippi Psychiatric Association. The Mississippi Psychological Association thinks, like all psychologists, that mental illness is a behavioral phenomenon only. But psychiatrists know that mental illness is a chemical disease of the brain that results in abnormal behavior, and or feelings, and only medication can fix it. They, the Mississippi Psychological Association, however run clinics in almost every county of the state. And Dr. Joe was privileged to work at a number of these facilities. There was always a psychologist in charge of each clinic. These clinics received both State and Federal funds on which to operate. They hired psychiatrists, usually those still in training, to do their work. The reason for this was that prescriptions had to be written for most of the mentally ill patients and only a medical doctor can write t hose prescriptions. (Nurse practitioners are also, these days, allowed to write some prescriptions, but there are limits on what and how much they can write.)

Dr. Joe found in the early going that the supervisors of these clinics want to see the patients back every month whether they needed to be seen or not. This really rubbed Joe the wrong way. When Dr. Joe told a patient to come back in 3 months and that was overridden by the supervisor of the clinic who told the patient to return in 1 month, Joe was greatly upset. Dr. Joe locked horns with the supervisor right then and there and ended up walking right off the job. This was and still is a constant abuse by the State Mental Health Clinics where Dr. Joe worked. It was wasteful and fraudulent for these State clinic workers to have patients returning every month when they are doing it for the sole reason of increasing the clinic revenue. This was the routine for all the clinics where Dr. Joe worked. And as a result of this, Dr. Joe parted ways with a number of these clinics because of this kind of waste, fraud and abuse. (This is really the reason why the State should not be involved in the healthcare business. If these patients paid their own healthcare bill they would come only when there was a need.)

Chapter 12
PSYCHIATRY PRACTICE NEAR MADISON, MS

DR. JOE WENT ON TO finish his 4 years of post graduate work in psychiatry in 1991. He then decided to open an office near his home in Madison, which was about 10 miles north of downtown Jackson. He had a friend and neighbor who owned a drugstore in downtown Madison and his friend had some undeveloped space behind his drugstore that could be made into an office. Joe rented the space and had it developed into a very nice office for psychiatry.

Author photo

THERE WAS ONE OTHER physician across the parking lot who was a family practice doctor. The use of the upstairs was a nice idea, except older patients had to walk up the stairs. However, most of Dr. Joe's patients would be children. He was there for one year, but the practice just wasn't working up to its full potential. The trouble, Joe thought, was that he was out on the periphery to the north and way out of the mainstream of patient flow. That's when he decided to pay the administrator of Barter Hospital a call. He did so, and the administrator agreed that he would be better off to relocate closer to the hospital. But he let Dr. Joe know up front that it was he, Dr. Joe, who needed the hospital, not the hospital who needed him. Joe had just met another man that was full of himself. Dr. Joe said, "Very well," and left.

It was maybe a day later that a psychiatrist by the name of Ronald Geld called Dr. Joe and asked if he would be interested in joining a group of four psychologists and one adult psychiatrist, saying that they had a child psychologist but needed an adult psychiatrist with child credentials. Joe agreed to talks. In the meantime he went to see an old friend, a female psychiatrist to ask her opinion. When they sat down in her office and Joe told her about the offer she said, "No, I would not go in with that group because Ronald Geld does not have a good reputation with the psychiatric community." She gave details, which Joe appreciated, and Dr. Joe thought about it a few more days. He also looked at other possibilities but all came up blank.

Finally after a few more weeks with no solution in sight Dr. Joe agreed to go into practice with Ronald Geld's group of the four psychologists and one adult psychiatrist. So he shut down his office 10 miles up the road and started anew with a group situation. Dr. Joe had always been in solo practice before and expectations of this new practice were dubious at best; and he knew he was going against the advice of his old friend.

Anyway, things were off to a roaring start. There were plenty of patients for him to see and he was busy. But a funny thing happened after the first month when the clinic divided up the money. Dr. Joe was paid about $2,000. He asked his colleague about this and it was explained to him that he would catch up in a few months, that it was just a quirk in the way the money was divided, and that it would all even out in a few months; something to the effect that these psychologists, whose fees and income were less, had to be helped along. To shorten the narrative a bit, things never got any better and finally Dr. Joe had had enough. He told the other psychiatrist who had hired him that he would have to leave. Dr. Joe separated his practice and began his own solo practice once again. Then Dr. Geld demanded that he vacate the office space. So Joe moved down to the Barter Hospital Outpatient space where he rented a suite of offices from the hospital.

While Dr. Joe was with that group practice he had seen a female patient of Dr. Geld's that was 33 years old, black hair, and just a little on the plump side. Dr. Geld was out of town and she came into Joe's office unannounced insisting on seeing him. Dr. Geld was treating her for anxiety and depression. As part of her history she volunteered that she was a Republican Party member and her function was entertaining out of town luminaries of the Republican Party when they were in town. Her home was in Vicksburg and her uncle was a high mucky muck in the Republican Party. That was the only contact Dr. Joe ever had with her. She tried to make other appointments with his office but he repeatedly refused to see her.

The next time Dr. Joe would hear from her would be through the State Medical Licensure Board where she claimed that he had made unwanted sexual advances towards her. Dr. Joe denied the allegations but the Medical Licensure Board was absolutely hysterical. Dr. Joe was adamant in defending himself but feminism had reared its ugly head and the board had to have a hanging. They had no evidence whatsoever, just a sick histrionic female to deal with. It didn't matter that they had no evidence, there was going to be a hanging. And Dr. Joe's ex-partner, who was angry with him for leaving the group practice, was all too happy to testify against him. Of course all Geld had to say is whatever she had told him. It was all fiction, everything he said was what she said, but the State Medical Board wanted that hanging since they had never had a case like this before.

Well, they had their monkey trial and without a shred of evidence Dr. Joe's license was suspended for one year. Dr. Joe was also sentenced to attend a special group in Atlanta for sexual deviants. Lisa was absolutely livid with anger. She had never seen anything like this among civilized people and knew that Joe was not a liar. But this was the Bible Belt. And what Dr. Joe's good friend had said proved to be absolutely true about this Ronald Geld person. He would stop at nothing to damage anyone who crossed him. (There has to be a way sometime when liars like Mr. Geld will get his just rewards for lying.)

So, Joe and Lisa flew to Atlanta once a month for a year. The whole group that Dr. Joe attended was really strange. They were totally normal appearing men. All were in the group for having committed, or having been accused of some grave sexual offense. And the offenses were serious for such otherwise healthy appearing people. For example, one man, about 30 years old, who sat next to Joe in one meeting, was there for molesting his wife's 6-year-old daughter by a previous marriage. Joe asked him what could be so appealing about a 6-year-old? His response was, "They are so pure, virtuous and untouched." And that was what turned him on. Not the girl's mother to whom he was married, but this pure, virtuous, 'white as the driven snow', 6-year-old. Though Joe was a licensed psychiatrist, he was totally dismayed.

Another case was a guy who was there for pulling his car up in the parking lots of grocery stores, opening his car door and masturbating when the female driver of another car approached or came near his car. He looked to see what reaction the scene created in the female victim. Can you imagine that? And all of this group of about 12 males were there for similar offenses. When Joe left the group meetings, which lasted for an hour on Friday afternoon, he and Lisa would laugh hysterically. It was really a fun group because Dr. Jim Sable, the doctor who conducted the group would zero in on one of these guys each week and make the whole group session that day about him. He never picked on Dr. Joe because he was all too aware of the questionable circumstances under which Joe was there.

Fortunately a year earlier Dr. Joe had bought a V35B Bonanza, tail number N1587L, so the monthly trip to Atlanta was much easier. Joe had installed a storm scope and a terrain map that greatly increased his capabilities regarding all weather flight. It also had the King Gold radio package with dual ILSs. Joe and Lisa flew in a lot of night weather; which he would not recommend unless you are a highly trained and skilled pilot.

Author photo

IN FACT, WHEN DR. JOE finished his one year out of practice, Dr. Sable allowed Dr. Joe to fly to Atlanta and pick him up to go to Jackson to testify before the Medical Licensure Board in his behalf when he was ready to resume his practice. Dr. Sable testified that Dr. Joe was psychiatrically healthy and a danger to no one. Dr. Sable knew from the start that this whole matter was a dirty hit job by a politically motivated licensure board; and went on to tell Dr. Joe that the only other licensure board in the U.S. that was more extreme and backward as the Mississippi board was the Iowa board.

Chapter 13
Guilty... Until Proven Innocent!

BUT THE HIT JOB DIDN'T end there. During the one year that Dr. Joe was out of practice the Mississippi State Attorney General was quoted as saying that if Dr. Joe ever came back into practice he was going to put him right back out of practice. This was extreme news to Dr. Joe as he didn't know anything about law; but he thought it highly unusual that a prosecutor would threaten anyone publicly in this manner. Joe had always been a staunch conservative and was never afraid to express his views. But was that a legitimate reason to go after him? (There you go Ned Noore, thumping on that bible again.) Within two weeks of Dr. Joe's resumption of his medical practice the attorney general had his people sent to the hospital to go through all of Dr. Joe's charts. No one had a clue as to what they were looking for.

The State took two months to review all Dr. Joe Ruff's charts dating back to when he first started his psychiatric practice. In all that time they found a total of 30 instances where there was a charge made but no progress note was written in the patients' charts. And of course everyone knows that any doctor can forget to write a note on occasion. Not to mention that this Attorney General was playing to the bible thumping base who are honest people, good people, but who don't understand the situation or the law and are being taken advantage of by an Attorney General who is totally without morals or scruples.

Now what was Dr. Joe charged with? He was charged with 30 FELONY counts for billing a patient without having seen them. **Felony meaning, you can go to prison for this.** Now how did this all come about?

The very next morning after the indictment of Dr. Ruff came out, a minority friend of Dr. Ruff's came rushing into his office. The doctor was very upset. The doctor said, "I have received word that the Attorney General was checking my practice as well." Dr. Joe asked, "Why the worry?" The doctor went on to say that he had been writing Ritalin prescriptions for children and letting the mothers of the children just stop by the reception desk at his office to pick up the prescription without seeing the patient. But he was still charging the child with an office visit. Dr. Joe was to learn later that the Attorney General's agents did visit that doctor and gave him a clean bill of health. Hard to believe. Right? Clean practice, no violations. Right?

Dr. Joe Ruff, not having been trained in law, knew nothing about how scurrilous a profession the practice of law really was. He inquired of his attorney as to a good criminal defense attorney and was referred to Jim Spaghetti, who was purported to be the one to see if you needed a criminal defense attorney.

Mr. Spaghetti met with Dr. Joe in the office of Joe's family lawyer to begin with, that is, when these indictments were handed down from a Grand Jury. Now if you know anything about Grand Juries, you would know that they will indict anyone for anything because the supposed criminal or his lawyer are not allowed to be present. **Really fair, right?** In common language, they can talk about you in private, indict you in private, and you nor your lawyer are allowed to be there. **Is that fair?** And according to a Supreme Court decision in 1992, prosecutors were not even required to present exculpatory evidence to the Grand Jury.

The first thing Dr. Joe asked Mr. Spaghetti was, "How much will you be charging?" His response was, "I would defend Murder One for

$25,000." In other words, that's the most it will cost. So Dr. Joe agreed to the deal.

The next scene was in Mr. Spaghetti's office at which time Mr. Spaghetti said, "We will need a special private detective to go through the 30 charts in question to see why you were indicted." The so-called expert didn't find anything wrong with any of the charts that would warrant any kind of charge.

Dr. Joe then said, "I will get my hospital administrator to testify as to the fact that theses patients were all seen on the day of the charge by residents." Mr. Spaghetti then responded with vigor, "Absolutely not! You are not to talk to anyone but me about your case or I will not be your counsel." Of course Dr. Joe had already paid the $25,000 up front, as demanded by Mr Spaghetti; and the next thing out of Mr. Spaghetti's mouth was, "And that will be another $600 for the investigator who went through the charts." To which Dr. Joe responded, "Well maybe he knows more about medical charts than I do, but I doubt it."

The very next appointment Dr. Joe had with Mr. Spaghetti was a month later. Mr. Spaghetti said, "You are going to need to go down to the county penal farm and be finger printed and photographed today." Dr. Joe was aghast and responded, "Why? I thought I was innocent unless I had been convicted?" Mr. Spaghetti said, "I don't know why, just go and do it because the Attorney General says you must. I will provide the transportation." His driver took Dr. Joe to the penal farm, where he was put through a half dozen locked gates and into a prison cell where he had to wait 2 hours. Then an armed guard came and took him to an area where he was finger printed and stood for a mug shot and then it was out the same half dozen locked gates and back to Mr. Spaghetti's office. Again Dr. Joe asked Mr. Spaghetti why this was done. He thought this procedure followed a guilty verdict. Spaghetti responded again that the Attorney General, Ned Noore, had ordered it. Mr. Spaghetti went on to say, "And I need another $10,000 from you." Dr. Joe protested, but Mr. Spaghetti said, "This has become a complicated case." So now the cost of being represented was $35,600 and Dr. Joe thought he had no recourse at this point.

When Joe got home and told Lisa what had happened, she was fuming. She called her Dad in Montana and talked with him about what was happening. They both agreed that this treatment was totally egregious and uncalled for in this instance.

Dr. Joe saw Mr. Spaghetti every month and after about another 4 months Mr. Spaghetti said, "The Attorney General has ordered you to go to the penal farm to be fingerprinted and photographed again." Dr. Joe protested but Mr. Spaghetti insisted he needed to comply. Joe again went through the same six locked gates, sat in a prison cell along with the inmates for a couple of hours, was finger printed and mug shot and released. He was angry by now and was slow to realize that he had been maneuvered into a trap; but now this man was $35,600 into his pocket.

During none of these visits did Mr. Spaghetti ever talk about the case in terms of what Joe's defense was going to be. Spaghetti seemed unconcerned about defending Joe's case. They never talked about who their side would call as witnesses or anything of the sort. Spaghetti scarcely ever mentioned the case. Dr. Joe thought this was odd but in all fairness he wasn't suppose to be an expert in law. All he knew about was medicine, and that was a full time job in itself. He had to trust his lawyer to represent his interest to the fullest extent of the lawyer's ability.

And the Attorney General took time to make a special film that aired on all of the TV stations about Dr. Joe's case, making sure that he could not get a fair trial, complete with a mug shot of the villain. And over the next several months Mr. Spaghetti continued to demand more money until Joe had paid him over $60,000. And at that point Dr. Ruff refused to pay him anymore.

Every month that Joe saw him, all Spaghetti would talk about was plea bargain. Joe told him every time, "Why should I plea bargain when I have broken no law?" Spaghetti simply appeared to ignore the issue.

Finally it was Friday before the trial date and Dr. Joe said, "What's our defense?" To which Spaghetti answered, "You must accept a plea bargain. Those criminals will murder you in prison when they find out who you are. You **must** accept a plea bargain!" Dr. Joe finally said, "Will I still be able to continue my practice and receive payment from medicare and other insurance carriers?" "Oh, yes," Spaghetti said. The doctor now knew that his lawyer, who was supposed to be on his side, was in fact an agent of the prosecution.

It was at that point that Dr. Joe stood up out of his chair and said , "YOU ARE FIRED, YOU NO GOOD THIEVING BASTARD!" He left and walked out onto the street.

Chapter 14
"Lisa, I Need You"

ON THE WAY HOME DR. Joe was fuming and decided he would rather have his wife, who was up to this time was practicing corporate law, defend him than be 'set up' this way. Although she had never tried a felony case, she'd defend him far better, rather than see him treated this way by a Jurisprudence System that had run completely out of control. He had previously decided not to involve her because he didn't want to put her under such stress; even though she had been telling him for months that she could defend him better than a crook like Spaghetti.

Lisa had suspected for a long time that she might have to jump in and defend Joe herself. She had been begging Joe to get rid of Spaghetti. So she had asked her Dad if he would arrange to get his license in MS so that he could assist her in case she had to try the case herself. So she and her Dad were ready when Joe finally gave in and came to her for help. It was decided that Lisa would try the case and her Dad would be her co-counsel. First Lisa and Dr. Joe got a delay to give her time to prepare the case. This would be Lisa's first real felony case in front of a jury. She said, "I know exactly how to win this case and we are going to do it."

Two months later it was now Lisa's time before the jury and this was her opening argument:

"Ladies and gentleman of the jury. My client and I understand the difficult position in which you have been placed. We only pray that you will give our defense the same credibility for which the prosecution is asking. Please keep an open mind about the things I am going to tell you about my client.

I have known Dr. Joe Ruff now for over 12 years. He has always been a kind and decent man and has never been involved with the law for any more than a traffic ticket. He has certainly been a wonderful and devoted husband and father. He is one of the few survivors of the Bay of Pigs Invasion of Cuba in 1961and nearly lost his life trying to return Cuba to democracy. He has served his country with honor. He has always been on the side of the law as long as I have known him. He has never wavered and has always kept his commitments to other people and this time is no exception.

I call my first witness to the stand to testify in this case, the Hospital Administrator of the Barter Hospital where all these alleged violations are said to have occurred, Mr. Earl Blassgame."

The bailiff called out, "Will Mr. Blassgame please take the stand."

The bailiff produced a Bible and asked Mr. Blassgame to put his hand on it and answer, "Do you swear to tell the truth, the whole truth and nothing but the truth, so help you God?"

Mr. Blassgame replied, "I do."

Lisa said, "Mr. Blassgame do you know the defendant?"

"Yes, he is a member of our hospital staff at Barter Psychiatric Hospital."

"Is he a member of the hospital in good standing?"

"Yes, certainly."

"Are you familiar with the charges against Dr. Ruff?"

"Yes."

"Were these 30 patients, who are alleged by the State as having no progress notes written, actually seen on the days in question?"

"Yes they were."

"Would you please explain to the ladies and gentlemen of the jury why no progress notes were written?"

"I have asked the resident physicians who saw the patients for Dr. Ruff on Saturday and Sunday why no progress notes were written and in each case they said they forgot to write them."

"Are those residents present in this courtroom?"

"Yes." "

Are they prepared to testify?"

"Yes."

Lisa called each of the residents to testify and their testimonies were the same as that of Mr. Blassgame's.

Lisa said, "Your honor I have no further questions. The defense rests."

The prosecutors tried desperately to get conflicting stories from all those who had testified, but failed.

The jury debated for 20 minutes and came back to the court room.

The Judge asked, "Have you reached a verdict?"

The Jury Foreman responded "We have your Honor. We the jury find the defendant, Dr. Joe Ruff, NOT GUILTY ON ALL 30 COUNTS."

Joe, Lisa and her Dad all hugged one another in jubilation over a victory where they knew all the political cards were stacked against them. Dr. Joe and Lisa decided they needed to be away from this kind of politics, so they moved away to Montana where Dr. Joe could practice his profession without further interference from a "cowboy" Attorney General like Ned Noore and where Lisa would be a partner in her Dad's law firm.

ADDENDUM

The Jurisprudence of America didn't just fall off a potato truck that happened to be coming through town. It was a long and thought out process that covered all of past history, but especially the last 200 years before the constitution of this great country was written. The laws of this country were carefully crafted after the concepts of old English law, which were crafted by the likes of Sir William Blackstone, an English jurist of the 18th century.

Blackstone taught that human rights and dignity were above the law. He also said that in order for a man to break a law he must know that he is breaking or violating the law. He said that it is part of the prosecutor's job to ascertain that an individual knew before the act that he or she was breaking the law. This is what the prosecutor has sworn to do as part of his Oath of Office.

In the case of Dr. Joe Ruff, the Attorney General, Ned Noore, either knew, or should have known, that he was violating Dr. Joe's rights by charging him with a crime when he knew, or should have known, that there was in fact no crime committed.

Mr. Noore, knew that Dr. Joe had committed no crime and that is why he pushed so hard for a plea bargain to begin with. He and Dr. Joe's own lawyer colluded against Dr. Joe. There never was any evidence of a crime. They both knew that and Dr. Joe knew it. The charge of a felony crime strikes fear in the heart of anyone so charged. That is a normal human reaction. But Mr. Spaghetti refused to even discuss Dr. Joe's innocence because he had a different agenda. Spaghetti's handpicked private detective could find no fault with Dr. Joe's charting. It was a simple matter of calling Dr. Joe's hospital administrator in to testify, but Mr. Spaghetti would not hear of it.

Dr. Joe had spent his entire life studying medicine and was totally unprepared to deal with two dishonest lawyers. He knew nothing about the law. And he simply didn't feel he could involve Lisa in this mess. When you are charged with a serious crime you don't stand a chance if both the prosecutor and your lawyer are colluding against you.

The plea bargain is the worst thing that has happened in American Jurisprudence since its beginning. A person gets charged with a crime they didn't commit and are offered a plea bargain. The way this works is that the person who is charged admits to a crime they didn't commit in order to get no jail time or a lesser sentence. That way the Prosecuting Attorney gets to beat on his chest over getting a conviction. And of course the best part is tomorrow's newspaper makes a hero of the Attorney General because he got a guilty plea for getting that dangerous criminal off the streets. Otherwise everyone has to go through the trauma of a full scale trial and no one knows for sure how that will turn out. So that's the bind in which Dr. Joe found himself. And that's not fair.

Ned Noore was a rogue prosecutor who had a reputation of prosecuting those who had broken no law. He was known to allow his own personal feelings and prejudice to dictate whom he charged with breaking the law, even though there was no crime committed. He was no different than the prosecutor who charged the Duke University LaCrosse team with a felony crime when they had not broken any law and in the process he savaged their lives and reputations. It is called **Prosecutorial Abuse or Misconduct!**

What does it mean if a prosecutor can indict you without having any evidence that a crime has been committed and then torture you until you admit to a crime that was not committed by you or by anyone; put you on trial and accept no evidence from you except your admission of guilt?

AUTHOR'S AFTERTHOUGHT

Not long after Dr. Ruff's case, the same Mr. Jim Spaghetti was brought into the local Hospital Emergency Room in a drunken stupor after he had fallen into his own rose bushes sustaining multiple bruises, abrasions and scratches. Indeed he was so drunk he could not communicate effectively. Would you want him to represent you in a Court where your whole life and everything you had worked all your life for was at stake?

And should any prosecutor have such power that he or she can decide subjectively whose career should be destroyed based on his or her own political or personal feelings?

Another thing: the only time the government ever offers a plea bargain is when they don't have the evidence to get a conviction.

And by the way, who is the person who was responsible for making mistakes in billing a FELONY offense, none other than the one and only Hillary Rodham Clinton in 1993. See how the law applies to just you but not to them? (the Clintons)

Don't miss out!

Click the button below and you can sign up to receive emails whenever P.T. "Doc" Carney publishes a new book. There's no charge and no obligation.

https://books2read.com/r/B-A-LHVF-GBVS

Also by P.T. "Doc" Carney

Joe Ruff's Exceptional Life
Hair On Fire in the 50s & 60s
Mississippi Justice: Guilty Until Proven Innocent!

About the Author

P.T. "Doc" Carney has entered the Golden Age of Retirement and is finally able to realize his dream of writing and publishing novels that he has envisioned for many years.

He is a retired USAF pilot, who entered as a cadet at the end of the Korean War and then flew with the Mississippi Air Guard for many years as a pilot and later as flight surgeon after receiving his medical license.

He grew up in rural Mississippi and as a child with ADHD was misunderstood for most of his childhood, as there was no diagnosis for ADHD at that time.

In his second book, Mississippi Justice: Guilty Until Proven Innocent, he continues the story of Joe Ruff as he returns from the Bay of Pigs Invasion fiasco to mend his body and his life and sets new goals for the future.

Read more at https://www.facebook.com/ptdoccarney/?ref=bookmarks.

About the Publisher

Doc and Eva Carney have been happily married for some 18 years now and Eva is so proud to be able to assist Doc with his publishing dreams. Few couples have experienced the togetherness that they still feel for one another today. "Soulmates" is the only term that applies.